I0737888

He Loves Me Not

Nenia Corcoran

Copyright © 2021 Nenia Corcoran

All rights reserved.

ISBN: 978-0-578-89384-6

TO JEFF

Thank you for your support, your encouragement and your love.

CHAPTER ONE

I can already tell I'm going to hate every minute of this process. You're asking me to bare my soul despite the fact we've only known each other for exactly eleven minutes. I've been watching the slow movement of the minute hand on your wall clock, designed to look like the paddle of a canoe against the slightly faded river scene.

It's sort of a cheesy clock, if you ask me, but everything in your office is pretty lame. It's almost like you're trying too hard to make it feel cozy. From the little wooden signs on the wall with cliché sayings about seizing the day and taking advantage of every opportunity, to the canvas paintings of sunsets over peaceful lakes. Your office basically screams "I'm a therapist trying to make you think you're comfortable!"

Here's a news flash: I'm not comfortable, and I sure as hell don't want to talk to you.

But since I'm being forced to sit here, I guess we might as well talk. Sitting here in silence would probably be just as awkward, and I know what you have to say about me is going to have a lot to do with whether they let me out of this place. I know I need the therapist sign-off to go home. I need you to say this was just a onetime episode and I can go back to being normal. I need you to believe I'm okay and everything is fine now, even if I'm not sure I believe it.

The days and weeks leading us to this room seem all fuzzy in my mind. It's like trying to recall the details of a dream that seemed so incredibly vivid at the time, but five minutes after you wake up, you're left with only wisps of vague concepts and nothing substantial enough to hold on to. When I look back at the last year of my life, I feel like all I have are those wispy details.

Obviously, I know I'm here to talk about Adam. I know that's what you're waiting for, as you tap that stupid gold pen against the page of your notebook. You want me to spill everything out and let the story flood your office. You're convinced putting the whole thing into words is supposed to help me somehow.

"We'll work through it together," you say cheerily, as if it's a difficult word problem written on the blackboard. But we weren't together through it all. I was alone, and just because you're sitting here with me now doesn't mean I don't still feel like I'm stranded on a deserted island.

You want me to give it a try. You're gently urging me to open up. You've probably practiced that look in the mirror, so it's just the right amount of concern paired with encouragement.

It's not easy, though, you know. I can't just put words to all the things that have been going on in my head for the past year. I don't even know if words exist within the English language for some of these feelings. I know you want me to try, but for Christ's sakes, don't you think I've been trying?

"Start at the beginning," you say, adjusting yourself in your seat. You cross your legs, one ankle over the other, and tuck them neatly behind the leg of your chair. It sickens me how professional you look, like the perfect image of a therapist on TV.

Pretty, polished, poised.

I bet you were always this pretty. Long blond hair that falls just perfectly into large ringlets around your face. I bet you try to pretend like you don't know how gorgeous you look, pulling your hair into a loose ponytail draped over one shoulder. The minimal makeup is a nice touch, too, an attempt at making it seem like you don't care too much about your appearance. But all you pretty girls are the same. Of course, you know how pretty you are. Pretty girls always know, even though they pretend they don't.

What you don't know, wouldn't even be able to begin to comprehend, is what it's like to be the other type of girl. The type of girl who isn't pretty or polished. The type of girl who tries so hard to make herself look acceptable, but always seems to come up short. I could never figure out how to tame my frizzy curls, and I sure as hell would never be able to make my ponytail look so effortless. I've spent the entirety of my teenage years battling the chaos that grows out of my scalp, and I've never once come up victorious.

Sitting here across from you, watching you use a manicured hand to toss your ponytail over your shoulder, I'm even more aware of the mane of flyaway curls that frame my face, despite the fact I've tried to slick my hair back into a tight French braid. As if having wild, untamable curls isn't bad enough, my hair is an obnoxiously bright red, which by its very nature draws attention to my inability to control it.

I resist the urge to reach up and flatten my fringe of rogue curls against my head. Instead, I just stare back at you, watching your cool blue eyes study me. I find myself briefly wondering if you're judging me, and I almost laugh out loud, realizing that's basically your job.

You ask me to start at the beginning like that's an easy location to find. I suppose for most people it is. The beginning is definable, the starting point of the story. But as I watch you watching me and listen to the tap of your pen against your notebook, I have no idea where that place could even be.

There isn't one specific moment that started everything. I can't pinpoint one day where everything changed. It's almost like I just woke up one morning and suddenly realized I had lost control.

Things had been set into motion at some point, and I was no longer capable of stopping them, and this is where we ended up. It doesn't feel like there was a beginning. It feels like there was a *before*, a *during* and a *now*. And it feels like there are different versions of me in each part. Like the me that's sitting here with you today isn't the same me that was there in the before part. She was a completely different girl. I don't even feel like I know that girl.

The Sasha of before would never have believed the Sasha of now could exist. And yet, here we are, you and I, sitting in your office with the stupid paddle ticking off the minutes we've been staring at each other. Twenty-seven minutes in, you stop tapping your pen and place it down on your notebook in your lap. You fold your perfect hands and say, ever-so-gently, "Sasha, I can't help you if you don't let me."

I let out a sigh. I know, Doc, that's the thing you don't get. You can't help me. I'm beyond help.

CHAPTER TWO

I'd been so certain high school would be a brand-new start for me. I thought I could shed the loser reputation I'd unfairly been branded with and start fresh. I could reinvent myself over the summer between eighth grade and high school and become the cool girl I dreamed about being. I was positive everything was going to be different when I entered Baymont High School.

Except it wasn't.

I was about to start my junior year and not a single thing had changed. It turns out, you can't just reinvent who you are. You can't erase an image of yourself from everyone else's mind and replace it with the image you want them to see.

So, despite the fact I'd spent that whole first summer coordinating cool outfits and practicing hair and makeup techniques I'd learned online, when I walked into school on the first day of ninth grade, no one looked at me any differently than they had the year before. I was still spineless Sasha, the nerdy girl who cried at the end of the documentary about baby turtles and accidentally told my math teacher I loved him at the end of class one day.

I kept up the fight to become popular through my sophomore year. I woke up at the crack of dawn and painstakingly straightened each and every strand of my frizzy, rebellious hair. I'd spend another thirty minutes slathering concealer over the gaggle of freckles that populated my cheeks and nose. I carefully selected my outfits based on the trends I studied on Pinterest. I put in all the effort, but no one seemed to notice. And by the end of the day, my hair would poof back up and my freckles would be shining through my cracking foundation.

I know I'm not pretty. We don't have to pretend I am for the sake of my self-confidence. My own mother didn't even try to hide the fact that, visually, I was a disaster.

"Maybe if you dyed your hair brown you would blend in better," she said.

Once, while I was waiting for her to pick up a prescription at CVS, I wandered over to the makeup aisle. I was looking at a display of deep red lipsticks, halfheartedly wondering what I might look like wearing such a dramatic color.

"Oh, God, no," my mother said, rounding the corner of the aisle and forcing me out of my daydream.

"Put that down, that's for the type of girl that can handle standing out in a crowd."

By the start of my junior year, I'd given up on the idea of changing my reputation. I stopped wasting time and energy on fixing my appearance, realizing no one was noticing me anyway. I accepted my place as a loser. The type of person who could sit next to you for an entire year in English class, and when asked my name, you wouldn't be able to recall it. Easily forgotten, only distinguishable as "that really smart redheaded girl."

That's why it came as such a shock, to everyone really, when Adam Lincoln sat down next to me on the first day of third-period chemistry.

Adam Lincoln was tall and effortlessly handsome. His brown hair was just a little too long, causing him to have to swipe it out of his eyes when he smiled. He was the catcher for the varsity baseball team and had been a star since his freshman year, when he made some amazing play that sent the team to the state championships for the first time in decades. Adam Lincoln was up there with the high school royalty.

When he walked into the room on the first day of chemistry, I obviously couldn't help but watch him. He glided into the room with the kind of effortless ease all popular kids possess. Do they teach that? Do they pull the pretty kids aside early on and teach them how to look so Goddamn perfect? Where I try to slink into a room hoping no one will notice me, Adam's presence basically commands attention. I watched him flip his hair out of his eyes as he surveyed the classroom in front of him like a king overlooking his subjects.

The stool next to me was unoccupied, which wasn't a surprise. Many of the stools were still available, as class wouldn't officially start for another three minutes. Everyone knew choosing seats on the first day of chemistry was a tactical decision. The two people sharing a station would be lab partners for the remainder of the year. Short of a death or an act of war, there was no changing seats or partners after today.

I anticipated my partner would be the unfortunate soul who happened to arrive last to class. I was secretly hoping perhaps there would be an odd number of students, thus sparing me the embarrassment of someone dropping their shoulders at the realization there were no more available spots and sliding onto the stool next to me as if they had just been handed a social death sentence.

But after glancing around the room, Adam Lincoln walked directly to my table. He smiled at me, and I couldn't help but notice how there appeared to be gold flecks floating in the brown pools of his eyes. I was so busy staring at him, I almost didn't realize he had spoken to me.

"Anyone sitting here?"

"Uh, no, no one is," I stammered, realizing I probably looked ridiculous gawking at him like that. Internally, I scolded myself while pretending to study the large poster of the periodic table hanging nearby. Adam slid onto the stool and dropped his backpack on the floor between us. I noticed a few of the other girls in the room glancing at our table, and I could have sworn they were glaring at me.

The rest of the stools around us filled up, and Adam acknowledged a few friends as they filtered into the room. I expected he'd get up and move his seat at the last minute, realize the mistake he'd made and run to safety before it was too late. When the bell rang, Mr. Carter closed the door and welcomed us all to class. He passed around a seating chart, and we all signed our names, chaining us to the seats we'd just selected.

I printed my name in delicate letters and slid the chart across the table to Adam. I held my breath, half expecting him to see my name printed on the paper and suddenly realize who I was. I waited for him to raise his hand and announce to Mr. Carter that there had been a mistake and he needed to change his seat.

But Adam just printed his name onto the chart next to mine and passed it on. I watched as the paper moved away from us, still struggling to believe Adam Lincoln had just willingly partnered himself with me for an entire year.

You must think I'm naïve, that I'm some kind of idiot for not realizing every kid in school knew a nerd like me would excel in chemistry. You've probably already figured out that Adam strategically chose his partner to ensure his chemistry grade was high enough to keep him on the baseball team.

Of course, I should have realized that the second he sat down, but honestly, it didn't dawn on me until several weeks later. By the time it did, it was already too late to turn back.

During our second class, we had our first lab assignment. It was a stupid worksheet, an intro-to-laboratory-work type of thing. The purpose was obviously to familiarize ourselves with the equipment and materials available to us. It was essentially a glorified scavenger hunt.

Only one worksheet was provided to each station. With the sheet between us, we set to work crossing off tasks as we completed them. Most of the tasks were so simple, they didn't require much discussion. Adam and I moved around each other, collecting the items on the list, practicing lighting Bunsen burners and arranging beakers across the desk.

There was only about five minutes left of class when I leaned down over the paper to read the last task. At that exact moment, Adam leaned in to cross off the task before it. Our shoulders bumped as his arm brushed against mine. I leapt back, nearly toppling my lab stool in the process. Adam smiled, his dimples making a sudden appearance as he continued to scratch off the number on the paper.

I felt my face begin to burn. Most girls look endearing when they blush, a soft pink filling the apples of their cheeks and making them appear sheepish and sweet. The heat was rising into my eyebrows, and I knew my face would be turning a blotchy, tomato red. I don't blush; my face ignites with a red-hot fire that sets my hair ablaze. The knowledge of how ridiculous I look when embarrassed only increases my embarrassment. It's a never-ending cycle that almost always ends with tears.

Adam didn't appear fazed by the inferno transforming my face. The last task on the paper required us to undo all the preparations we had done for the fake lab. We had to return our materials to their places and clean up our workspace. Adam collected all the equipment he could carry and transported them to the back of the room. Luckily, by the time he returned, I'd suppressed the urge to cry enough to force myself to help with the task. With my head bent in an attempt to mask my still-obvious embarrassment, I cleared away the last of the materials and scrubbed down the tabletop, despite the fact that we hadn't actually done anything that might have required scrubbing.

Adam looked over the worksheet and handed it to me for final approval. He grinned and asked me if I thought we'd get an A on our first assignment. I stared down at the paper, contemplating if he was seriously doubting whether we properly completed the fake assignment. It was essentially the easiest thing we would do all year, and it certainly hadn't taken any amount of skill or expertise. Before I could determine if he was joking, the bell rang.

Adam slipped gracefully off his stool and slung his backpack over one shoulder. He raised his hand in a wave as he sauntered out of the classroom and was engulfed by the storm of kids pressing through the hallway. I stared after him, finally deciding that he had, in fact, been joking.

CHAPTER THREE

I know what you're thinking. I'm pathetic. It's true, of course. But someone like you will never be able to understand what it's like to be a loser. I wasn't prepared to be wittily bantering back and forth with one of the most popular boys in the junior class. There aren't any books that you can study to tell you how to properly engage in a conversation with a teenage boy. At least, not in our library.

Luckily for me, or maybe unluckily based on how things all turned out, Adam wasn't immediately put off by my obviously delayed social skills. I've always wondered whether he knew right away he was going to choose me, or if it was something that just sort of happened, some opportunity he decided to take advantage of. Was my vulnerability obvious early on or was it something he realized he could take advantage of? I've asked myself that question a thousand times through the nights I've been here, lying awake and staring at the stucco ceiling.

I wasn't popular, but I guess I wasn't a social outcast either. I had a group of friends I felt comfortable with. It's not like I had to sit alone in the lunchroom; I just wasn't getting invited to Nancy Molton's infamous Sweet Sixteen party at her parents' lake house.

My best friend, Amanda Attwood, was the polar opposite of me. She was chatty and outgoing. She loved being the center of attention and had no fears about being on stage. She dreamed of being a Broadway star and was not going to let the fact that she was a size sixteen deter her from reaching her goal. She wasn't necessarily classically beautiful, but she certainly had the attitude of an actress.

Amanda and I would sit at our lunch table with our collection of friends, and I would listen to her loudly share her opinions, always envious of the ease with which she commanded the table. I would sit quietly and eat, conscious of the fact that even among our friends, I was fading into the background.

But if I'm being honest, the background suited me just fine. The further into the background I faded, the less I was concerned about my frizzy hair or lack of social skills. As a casual observer of what was happening around me, I was comfortable.

I'm sure in your shrink book that speaks a lot about my character. I think the term is introverted, but I don't think there's anything wrong with being introverted. I'm comfortable in situations I'm familiar with. What's so bad about that?

You prompt me to keep going. You're tapping your pen again. Maybe I'm boring you. I know you want the juicy details about what happened between Adam and me. You probably want to hurry up and get to that part so you can write your fancy shrink words down in your notebook and call it a day. You'll lock me up in the loony bin so I'm no longer a danger to myself or others and then move on to your next patient without even batting one of those perfectly outlined eyes.

I know what you're looking for. But the thing is, I don't know when the thing with me and Adam went so bad. It feels like one day it just was. One day I didn't have Amanda anymore. I didn't have the safety of my lunch table or the group of other nerds to blend in with. One day I didn't have anything at all.

One day, I was just suddenly someone else.

I know you don't want to hear about it, but I think the fact that Amanda is so outspoken is important to the overall story. I think that's why Adam never liked her. She wasn't enchanted by his reputation or his good looks. She challenged him all along, pushed his buttons whenever she could. Now that I think about it, maybe she was fighting for me and I just couldn't see it at the time.

I wish I could go back to the first time Amanda said she didn't like Adam. I wish I could hear what she said then with the knowledge of what I know now. I wish I hadn't gotten so mad at her. There aren't many things I regret more than the day I accused her of being jealous of me. I know I said some terrible things. I can't take them back, but I hope I get a chance to apologize for them.

I wonder if it would have changed everything if just once I had listened to her instead of defending Adam. I wonder if she could have saved me.

No. I know that sounds stupid. I'm sure the reality is that no one could have saved me. But maybe if I'd listened better at the time, I could have saved myself.

But I can't help but wonder how she knew. How could she see the things that I couldn't see?

How was I so blind?

CHAPTER FOUR

I told Amanda that Adam Lincoln chose me to be his lab partner at lunch that first day. She frowned and asked if I was upset that I'd gotten such a shitty partner. Of course not, I told her, I didn't think he was a shitty partner.

"He's not very smart," Amanda pointed out as we set our trays down in our usual places. I reminded her I hardly needed help passing a basic chemistry class. Amanda simply shook her head before launching into a debate with Andrew about what the feature play should be that fall. Like every season, Amanda wanted the show to be *Grease* so she could play the part of Sandy. She absolutely adored the Sandy role, though I had some doubts Amanda would be able to pull off the slinky bodysuit Sandy wears at the end of the musical when she sings "You Better Shape Up."

Over the next several chemistry classes, I worked up to a certain comfort level with Adam. I went from not even being able to form sentences when he asked me a direct question to being able to offer information to him without turning the color of a fire engine. I was even starting to catch on when he was making jokes.

I would say I got comfortable working with Adam only because

I was comfortable with the work. Chemistry came easily to me, and I could force that to be the focus. Adam and I rarely talked about anything but the tasks at hand, which was fine by me.

About two weeks into the school year, Adam complimented me on the emerald-green shirt I was wearing.

"That color looks good on you; you should wear it more often."

Immediately my face flamed. The flush started extending out toward my ears. I buried my face in my textbook, thankful for the fact that Mr. Carter was lecturing today and there was no further reason for Adam and me to interact. Even though I was boring holes into my textbook with my eyes, my brain was thoroughly distracted with unrelated thoughts.

Adam Lincoln thinks this color looks good on me I thought over and over. I had already mentally sorted through the rest of my wardrobe. I didn't own anything else quite this color. I made the decision to order as many emerald-green tops as I could find on Amazon as soon as I got home. I'd delayed back-to-school shopping, so I felt like I could justify ordering a few things without feeling guilty.

When I relayed the compliment to Amanda later that afternoon, she wrinkled her nose.

"What does he know?" Amanda said. "There are lots of colors you look good in. Personally, and I've told you this a thousand times, I think you look amazing in purple." Despite what Amanda thought, I purchased eight emerald-green tops in various styles later that night.

From that day on, I wore emerald green to nearly every chemistry class. Only once did Amanda mention the fact that I was now wearing emerald green nearly every other day.

"Don't you think you're overdoing it a little on the green?" she asked one morning when I came in wearing yet another new green top. "It's like you're turning into a leprechaun or something."

Instinctively, I ran my hands over the fabric, smoothing it against my skin.

"I like it," I said, more defensive than I intended to sound. Amanda raised an eyebrow.

"Do you?" she asked.

I didn't answer, and I don't think she needed me to. The bell rang, and we went our separate ways.

If Adam noticed the immediate effects of his comment on my wardrobe, he didn't mention it. I was a little disappointed that he never complimented me again, despite how many different emerald-green shirts I came to class in. Regardless, I was happy with the fact that Adam and I were working quite nicely together. Halfway through the first term, he was thrilled to share with me that this was the highest his science grade had ever been.

"Coach is going to be so proud when I tell him I pulled this off."

Adam was studying our latest lab score. The bright red A scrawled across the top of the page was no surprise to me. I asked him if he normally struggled with science, and he told me he'd nearly failed last year. He explained his coach had needed to arrange an extra-credit assignment for him so he could play in the state championships. I had no idea you needed to maintain a certain grade-point average to remain on a sports team's roster. Suddenly, all the light bulbs in my head were turning on at the same time.

"Oh." I was unable to hide the bitterness in my voice. "I guess that explains why you partnered with me. You just needed to get a good grade." Adam looked up at me, the smile falling from his face.

"No, Sasha, of course not. I like you, and I thought we'd work well together." He put his hand on my shoulder, and I wonder if he noticed that I flinched when he did so. It was so natural, but the sudden contact made my vision blur. Tears pooled in the corners of my eyes, but I was determined not to let him see. I turned away from him as I fought them back.

"Come on, Sash," he said as he gently squeezed my shoulder. "You know it's not like that between us. We're friends."

My brain snapped to attention at the word. I turned and stared at him, sure I must have heard him wrong. But there he was, sitting next to me, his arm draped casually across my wilted shoulders. I straightened and smiled, trying to play off my moment of weakness.

"Sure, I know."

I forced a smile, and Adam brightened. He turned his attention back to the graded paper in front of him, and I tried to focus on what Mr. Carter was writing on the white board.

The whole thing left me unsteady. In what world would I have known that Adam Lincoln and I were friends? He was absolutely everything I was not. He was athletic and popular and charming and handsome. I didn't even know if Adam Lincoln had actually known my name prior to this class, and now he was saying we were friends? I couldn't help but feel a little lighter after that.

CHAPTER FIVE

Yeah, it was naïve. In fact, it was straight-up idiotic. Of course the reason that Adam Lincoln sat down next to me on the first day of chemistry was because he needed to get a good grade. Amanda was the first one to tell me I was falling for a load of crap. In fact, those were her exact words. She spent nearly two weeks insisting he was using me for my grades.

"Sweetie," she said, a pet name she only deployed when trying to soften the blow of her blunt words, "you're a straight-A student with an affinity for science. He's using you, and you're totally eating it up."

"Quit being so dramatic." I hated that she couldn't just be happy for me. "It's not like this is one of your TV shows where kids from different cliques can't be friends."

Amanda bit her lip, a restraint tactic she usually used to prevent her tongue from getting her in trouble. She forced a small smile and said, "Yeah, you're right." She turned back to her lunch, and I didn't attempt to argue any further. I knew there was more she wanted to say. I knew Amanda better than to think she would actually give up that easily, but part of me was hoping she was wrong. I wanted to believe that Amanda was just being overly skeptical.

I guess I just wanted to believe it was possible that Adam and I could be misunderstood friends. I've seen it happen before in some of those very TV shows I chastised Amanda for watching. Surely there was the chance, despite our different social standings, that Adam and I could have a friendship that existed within the realm of chemistry class.

Even I wasn't naïve enough to fathom our friendship could survive being subjected to the real world. I couldn't just walk up to him in the halls and strike up a conversation. I didn't want to know what Adam might do if I approached him while he was surrounded by his popular friends or teammates. But within the confines of our third-period chemistry classroom, I truly believed it was possible for us to be friends, regardless of what Amanda said.

What's that say about me, Doc? Am I a fool? Am I that desperate to be liked? Probably.

But as things progressed between Adam and me, I dared to think I was actually proving Amanda wrong. I was sure that I was breaking the stereotypical mold and that Adam and I were the exception to the clearly-defined rules of the high-school food chain. As the year marched slowly forward, I became more and more convinced.

During a lab just before Thanksgiving break, my skin prickled with goosebumps. I was wearing an emerald-green short-sleeve top, and despite the chilly weather, I'd neglected to bring a jacket to class. I didn't own anything long-sleeved in the emerald-green color Adam liked, and I hadn't justified another shopping spree. I hadn't anticipated how cold the chem lab would be.

I rubbed my arms between instructions, attempting to fend off the goosebumps. Adam hunched over the desk, his hand cupping his chin as he concentrated on the instructions in front of him. He glanced at me through the hair that fell in his face.

"Are you cold?"

"Oh, no. I mean, well, yes. I just forgot my jacket."

Adam reached down and untangled his black varsity baseball sweatshirt from his backpack. He held it out to me in a crumpled ball. I stared at it, hanging between us. I was confused. He jiggled his arm slightly, causing one of the sleeves to fall into my lap.

"Take it," he urged. "There's no point freezing for the whole class."

The sweatshirt felt heavy in my hands as I took it from him. I held it in my lap, staring at the embroidered Baymont High School logo. This felt so intimate. I knew his last name was embroidered on the sleeve. The girlfriends of various players proudly walked around the hallways in these oversized sweatshirts, staking their claim to the names printed on the sleeves. To the best of my knowledge, no other girl ever had the opportunity to wear Adam's name.

I pulled the sweatshirt over my head and felt its warmth envelop me. It smelled of stale cologne and sweat, but it wasn't necessarily an offensive odor. In fact, the scent made me feel a little lightheaded. As my face emerged through the neck hole and back into the harsh light of the classroom, I had the sudden urge to disappear into the sweatshirt again, like a turtle hiding from the outside world. I adjusted the bulky material around me and stole a peek at Adam. He seemed unfazed by this significant moment. He was back to staring down at the instructions in front of him, puzzling over one of the most basic questions on the page.

I looked around to see if anyone else was watching, and when I saw no one was, I quickly brought the sleeves of the shirt to my face and inhaled. I imagined this was what it would smell like to have Adam's strong arms wrapped around me, my face buried against his muscular chest. I was lost in this thought when Adam turned toward me and asked me about the lab. I ripped myself from my careless daydreams and tried to focus on the task in front of us, but my eyes kept wandering down to my right arm, where I could read "Lincoln" in white embroidered script.

When the bell rang, I stood to pull the sweatshirt off. I was lifting the hem when Adam shook his head.

"Keep it for the day," he said, scooping his bag off the ground. "I'll be in the gym after school. After you get your jacket, drop it off to me down there."

Adam disappeared into the hall without another word. I stood there in disbelief. My hands were still on the hem of the sweatshirt, ready to pull myself out of this dream. I blinked a few times, trying to wrap my head around what had just happened. I might have stood there forever, but Mr. Carter interrupted my thoughts, asking if I was all right. I nodded and gathered my things. I rushed out of the classroom, determined to show Amanda how wrong she was before the magic of the moment wore off.

I practically strutted up to where Amanda was standing outside of the lunchroom. I positioned myself so that she couldn't help but notice the name on the sleeve of the sweatshirt. I watched with giddy excitement as her eyes lingered over the letters.

I eagerly awaited her response. I expected my best friend to launch into an enthusiastic apology for ever doubting my relationship with Adam. I was ready to forgive her and desperate to discuss what receiving the sweatshirt might mean. I was dying to ask her if she felt this was as serious as I thought it was. Adam Lincoln had given me his sweatshirt to flaunt in the hallways, for Christ's sake. I was practically bubbling over with emotions.

But Amanda didn't apologize. She didn't even acknowledge the sweatshirt. She adjusted her bookbag on her shoulder and casually asked me if I had notes on *Pride and Prejudice*.

I stared at her, blinking, trying to process what she'd said.

"What?"

"Didn't you take notes on *Pride and Prejudice* last year? I know you still have them. You never throw your notebooks away."

"*Pride and Prejudice*? What does that have to do with anything?"

"I was supposed to read it, but I've been so busy with the play. I just want to glance through your notes for essay topic ideas." I couldn't wrap my mind around this shift of topic. I was certain Amanda had seen Adam's sweatshirt. We were together before school started; she knew what I was wearing this morning. Why wasn't she as excited about this new development as I was?

"Do you not see what I'm wearing?"

"I see it. Can I come by for those notes tonight after rehearsals?"

"Yeah, sure, whatever." I fluttered my hand, trying to sweep away the nonsense Amanda was talking about. "Isn't this amazing?" I lifted my right arm toward her in case she hadn't fully grasped that it was Adam's last name on the sleeve. Amanda rolled her eyes.

"You want me to be impressed by the fact that you're wearing his dirty sweatshirt?"

My excitement deflated. The heat was rising in my cheeks.

"He gave it to me because I was cold."

"What was wrong with your jacket?"

"Nothing." I was getting defensive. I hugged my arms around my stomach, unconsciously pulling Adam's sweatshirt tighter around me. "I didn't have my jacket in chem. Adam gave me this to keep warm."

"Well, don't forget to give it back."

The bell rang, and Amanda took a step toward the hall before changing her mind. "Sweetie," she said, softened, and I hoped it was concern and not pity I was seeing in her eyes. "It's all an act. He's really good at looking good." She patted my arm and disappeared into the sea of students forcing their way through the narrow halls.

When I arrived at my last class, I couldn't concentrate on anything going on around me. For what was maybe the first time in my school-attending life, I zoned out for an entire period. When the final bell rang, I still hadn't cleared the thoughts from my head. All I kept wondering was why Amanda was so against my relationship with Adam. I was also aware that each time I pondered this question, I felt a little thrill at the idea of using the term "relationship" to describe what Adam and I had.

CHAPTER SIX

I honestly wouldn't have believed you if you told me two years ago that we'd be sitting here discussing my relationship with Adam Lincoln. I would have laughed in your face. What would a guy like Adam Lincoln want with a frizzy-haired nobody like Sasha Collins? To be honest, I still don't know the answer to that question.

Before Adam, I hadn't exactly been actively trying to find a boyfriend, but it wasn't like I was a prude either. I was interested in trying things out; it just didn't seem like any of the boys at Baymont High School were interested in trying those things out with me. Although sometimes I wondered if I was destined to be alone forever, being single did make it easy to find time for studying, and at least when I was studying my mother seemed pleased with me.

"How's my little bookworm?" she said as she brought fresh coffee into my room one night. I was cramming for a calculus test, though it turned out I hardly needed the extra hours of studying to pass with flying colors. After placing the steaming mug on the corner of my desk, my mother stood over me, affectionately stroking my curls. She peered over my shoulder at the textbook and gawked at the formulas I was scrawling across my notebook.

"You truly amaze me," she said after a while. "I was never good with all this numbers stuff."

"It's just filling in the blanks, Mom." I was used to this compliment. It's one of the few my mother fed me. Never once had she complimented me on an outfit or told me I looked nice, but she applauded me on my ability to study at least twice a week.

My mother clicked her tongue at my dismissal. "Don't forget to thank me in your Nobel Prize acceptance speech," she said as she headed toward the door.

I'm almost positive my mother has no idea what Nobel Prizes are awarded for. I'm even more positive my mother only cares about the Nobel Prize because she found out there's a cash prize associated with it. She doesn't really want me to thank her in my acceptance speech. She wants me to thank her with a payout. At least if I end up making her some money, she can justify having had me.

I've always known I was a disappointment to my mother. She was a cheerleader in high school and the homecoming queen two years running. She talks about high school like it was yesterday, as if she only just graduated and was still the most popular girl in town.

I guess, compared to some of my friends' parents, high school wasn't that long ago for my mom. She was a freshman at a community college when she got pregnant with me. She never talks about who my father might have been. Based on some of the stories I've heard about my mother, he could have been almost anyone. My mother is beautiful, and she liked to say that beautiful girls don't have to settle for just one man.

Although some people might have thought getting pregnant would put a cramp in my mother's pageant-girl style, my mother was an adorable pregnant woman. In the pictures I've seen, it looks more like she's got a balloon stuffed up her shirt than an actual human growing inside her. She was the most adorable type of pregnant, and it somehow made her look even more beautiful.

I know how thrilled she was when she found out she was having a daughter. She must have imagined all the ways she'd get to relive her glory days through her precious baby girl. When I was born, she entered me in all those baby beauty contests. There are hundreds of photos of me as a chubby, bald baby in various frilly outfits from these competitions.

What is the criteria to win a baby beauty contest, anyway? If you ask me, babies pretty much all look alike. There aren't a whole lot of babies that aren't cute. I probably looked exactly like ninety percent of the other babies entered in these contests, but I never brought home any baby crowns for cuteness. Thus beginning my mother's drawn-out disappointment in me as a daughter.

I often wonder what my mother's first thoughts were when I went from being a bald baby to a baby with crazy, curly, red hair. My mother has naturally beautiful chestnut-brown hair that falls in gentle waves around her shoulders. She prides herself on the fact she's never had to dye it to achieve this look.

Do you think she was shocked when she first noticed the wisps of red taking over my head? Of course, when I was a baby, my red curls were fine and soft. It wasn't until I got older that they became the frizzy mess they are today. Though I know my mother must have the recessive gene buried inside her DNA, I like to believe that I got the redhead gene from the man who donated his sperm to create me. Somewhere out there, there must be a man with unfortunate red hair that looks just like mine.

When I was six, my mother started me in gymnastics and dance classes to prepare me for what she assumed was my inevitable future as a cheerleader. There are dozens of photographs of my first few days in each program. My mother dressed me in brightly-colored leotards and pinned my curls up into pigtails and brought me to the classes. I don't remember much about them, but according to my grandmother, they were highly entertaining.

Grandma June would tell anyone who'd listen about my lack of coordination. She said it was apparent almost instantly, and I only made it about a month before my dance teacher told my mother I was a lost cause. Grandma June would howl with laughter at the memory of Madame Garrett trying to explain to my mother that continuing my enrollment in dance was simply a waste of my mother's money and Madame Garrett's time.

"Some kids have it," Grandma June said, "and some kids get thrown out of dance class."

Despite my lack of coordination, my mother was not prepared to give up on her hopes of molding me into the picture-perfect daughter she envisioned me to be. When I was ten, she signed me up for the local cheer squad. There wasn't a whole lot of skill involved It's not like they expected a whole bunch of fancy flips and kicks. They mostly just wanted me to be able to remember the words to the cheers and clap along to the beat.

Unfortunately, I never seemed to master the rhythm part of the cheers. To this day, I can recite most of the cheers word for word, but for some reason, clapping along to the beat completely escapes me. I guess you could say I'm just not musically inclined. And since I was the only redhead on the team of seven, I stuck out like a sore thumb when I was clapping ridiculously out of sync.

It wasn't long after that season that my mother finally gave up on me following in her footsteps. Even at ten, I could see how disappointed she was in the way I'd turned out.

"She didn't get that from me," she would say whenever one of my flaws was pointed out in public. She also never mentioned who it was that I might have gotten it from. Maybe that person would have been less disappointed.

Luckily, I was smart, and mom did love that I was the best at something. I won all the nerdy stuff in elementary school. Spelling bees, geography tournaments, math Olympics, all of those geeky things came easily to me. While I hated being up on stage to compete, I couldn't help but be happy that Mom was so proud of me while I was up there. Whenever I brought home a ribbon or a medal, it almost felt like I wasn't the biggest disappointment in her life.

I know we're not here to talk about my mother, though I feel like mothers always come up in therapists' offices. Are there people out there in the world who don't blame their mothers for the way they turned out? I know what happened between Adam and me isn't my mother's fault. She's just one more person I couldn't make happy.

CHAPTER SEVEN

My mother loved Adam from the first time she met him.

When she opened the door to find Adam standing there, she didn't bother to hide her shock that a boy of clearly superior good looks had shown up on our doorstep. His visit was strictly business, which I explained three times to my mother before his arrival, but she doted on him like he was a potential suitor anyway.

We sat in the kitchen with my notebooks and several textbooks strewn across the table around us. My laptop was open on the table which I had carefully cleaned up prior to Adam's arrival. I changed my desktop picture from the goofy photo of Amanda and me slurping ice-cream cones from the previous summer to a more sophisticated image of a sunset I'd taken on a camping trip a few months earlier. I'd tucked away all the personally-named files and ensured that none of the Internet tabs I'd left open would reveal anything embarrassing about me.

We were researching different uses for iodine as part of our thesis project. Adam had shown up twenty minutes after he said he'd arrive. He was sweaty and carrying his baseball bag. I was surprised, seeing as it was barely December. I hadn't realized that baseball was an all-year activity. He grinned and told me it only was if you were good.

Mom ushered him into the kitchen and offered him every drink in our fridge. He politely declined, holding up a half-finished Gatorade and stating that he was all set. He hadn't come with his own laptop, or even any of his notebooks. He simply settled in beside me at the table and started aimlessly flipping the pages of the nearest book.

It was obvious that Adam was clueless on how to write a thesis. His suggestions were mostly useless, and I found myself having to ignore them. After a while, he stopped offering any suggestions at all.

At one point, I pushed my computer aside and heaved one of my larger texts into my lap. As I was scanning it, Adam pulled my laptop toward him. He minimized our thesis and found himself staring at the sunset picture.

"Wow, this is a really cool shot."

I shrugged, trying to pretend I hadn't selected one of my favorite images for this exact reason.

"Thanks," I said, trying to sound casual. "It took me almost an hour to get the lighting just right."

Adam looked up, the surprise evident on his face.

"Wait, you took this?"

I nodded. I'd received a DSLR camera for my birthday two years prior. Photography had quickly become a passion. I had the patience to wait for the perfect shot. Sometimes that meant sitting with my tripod set up for hours. I didn't mind lugging my equipment around with me and holding out for the sun to be just right. It was my very own version of the thrill of the chase.

Adam studied the image on the screen. "Do you have more?"

"Sure." I clicked open a folder, and Adam began scrolling through the images. There were sunsets and sunrises, the fireworks over the Tugaloo River, some close-ups of flowers and some action shots of various animals. This folder was where I kept all of my favorite images. Nothing but my best work. I was thrilled to have the chance to show it off. The only other person who had ever admired my photos was Amanda.

The last photo in the album was an adorable image of Amanda's little brother, Ben. Ben is about six in the photo; it's from one of his first tee-ball games. He's wearing a blue baseball shirt and a dirty red batting helmet that's too big for his head. He has a wide grin on his face as he rounds the bases, his front teeth noticeably absent. It's one of my few photos with a human subject.

Adam stared at the picture, and I couldn't help but feel self-conscious, even though it was one of the ones I was most proud of.

"Will you come take photos like this at my games?" Adam asked without taking his eyes off the screen.

I immediately assumed he was joking or teasing me about my lame hobby. Over the past few months, I'd gotten fairly good at figuring out when Adam was joking, but when I looked at him, he actually seemed earnest. I nodded. I was surprised how excited I was when he smiled.

Mom came in to offer us snacks at least nine times during the two-and-a-half hours that Adam was in my kitchen. I say "us," but she was really only offering Adam snacks. He declined each time, and I could see the familiar look of disappointment on her face when Adam also declined her offer to stay for dinner.

"I should probably get going, actually," Adam said, glancing out the window. "I don't like to run after dark."

"Run? Did you run here?" My mother perked up. While clearly disappointed Adam wasn't going to stick around, this blatant show of manliness intrigued her.

"Yeah," Adam said, gathering up his baseball bag and pulling it onto his shoulders. "I live about two miles away, I figured this was a good way to get some cardio in after my workout with the team." I hadn't realized that Adam lived nearby. I guess I had no reason to know where he lived. After all, the only reason he knew where I lived was because I'd written my address down for him on Friday afternoon.

"I'll come by at two tomorrow afternoon," he said, not even bother to ask me if I had any other plans for the day. I mean, I didn't, but still, he should have asked, right?

From the kitchen window, I watched Adam jog down the street, his baseball bag bobbing up and down with each step.

"That's an impressive young man," my mother said, coming up behind me to watch Adam disappear around the corner onto the main road. I didn't respond. I knew my mother was fishing to see my interest level. Instead, I shrugged and set back to work, seeing as there was still a lot to do before our thesis was ready to hand in on Monday morning. Overall, I spent about seven additional hours on our project, apart from the few that Adam sat with me.

You're jotting things down as I talk, and I can't help but wonder if that's a good or a bad sign. As long as I keep spitting out words, you don't talk very much. Every once and a while, you look up from your notebook and smile at me, encouraging me to keep going. But I wonder whether I'm giving you good or bad evidence.

Am I proving to you that I'm crazy? That I was stupid to fall for all of this and I deserve to be locked up? Or am I showing you it wasn't my fault, that I didn't see what was in front of me and that I ended up here by accident?

On second thought, I don't know which is worse.

CHAPTER EIGHT

After the afternoon Adam let me borrow his sweatshirt, Amanda and I didn't talk about him for a while. It wasn't like I was purposely avoiding the topic; it just seemed like everything went smoother when we didn't talk about him.

Okay, fine. Maybe that's the very definition of avoiding a topic. But it was just easier to avoid it.

Two weeks before Christmas break, Amanda and I were sprawled across the floor in her bedroom surrounded by wrapping paper, ribbons, and gift bags. We had just returned from our annual trip to the mall where we purchased the gifts we would give to our family and friends. For the past several years we'd made a day of the event, shopping and then staying up to wrap our treasures, capping off the evening with cookie baking and cocoa.

I loved being at Amanda's at Christmas time. Christmas in my house was really just another day. We put up a tree and exchanged presents and participated in the expected traditions, but in the end, it wasn't really a big deal. Usually, once the gifts had been opened, we'd disappear to our own corners of the house, and we wouldn't interact again until dinner.

Christmas at Amanda's house was a month-long celebration, and every day was better than the last. They didn't just put up one tree; they put a tree in practically every room of the house. Amanda even had a small tree in her bedroom. The decorations didn't stop at trees. The Attwoods strung lights from every available surface. There were paper chains and popcorn strings around every doorway. The windows were all covered in paper snowflakes, and the living room was dominated by a village of tiny snow-covered model houses. Decorations spilled into the yard to include a giant inflatable Santa waving at those passing by on the street.

The festive atmosphere was not just limited to the house, either. All of the Attwoods embodied the attitude of eager elves during the month of December. There was a never-ending supply of Christmas cookies, and the carols began playing the day after Thanksgiving. It was the closest thing I could imagine to actually living in Santa's village.

"Did you buy that scarf for your mom?" Amanda pointed to the fake cashmere infinity scarf I was trying to figure out how to fold. The deep purple fabric shimmered as I twisted it in an attempt to force it to lie flat. I gave up my attempts and held it in front of me

"No, I was thinking my grandma might like it." Grandma June had recently acquired an affection for covering her neck. She was embarrassed of the age spots that were beginning to stand out against her pale, Irish skin. Amanda nodded her approval.

"She'll love it. I hope this sweatshirt isn't too small for Ben. Now that I'm looking at it, it seems awfully tiny."

She spread a camo-printed sweatshirt out across her legs. There was a black shadow of a soldier on the front. Ben was in an Army Man phase. The sweatshirt did look small lying on Amanda's legs, but when she had held it up in the store, I had been sure it would fit her little brother.

"What size is it?" I asked, finally deciding to stuff the infinity scarf into a gift bag rather than fold it. "We could go check the tags on some of his other sweatshirts to make sure."

Amanda checked the tag. "It's a youth medium. I guess that should fit. It just looks so little!" She folded the sweatshirt with the ease of someone who worked in retail. While at the mall, the only store that Amanda refused to enter was Forever 21, where she was currently employed. "We don't need any of that crap today, anyway," Amanda had said as we hustled past the glass windows in front of the store.

I imagined Amanda would later purchase me a top from Forever 21, using her employee discount. She only referred to the items inside as crap so she could avoid having to enter the store on her days off. She feigned hatred for the store and all of her coworkers, but I knew that she secretly loved it there. It was the perfect place to put her acting skills to work as she paraded around telling customers how wonderful they would look in garments they had no business wearing.

Amanda leaned against her bed and pulled her blond hair into a messy bun. I always envied the effortless way she did this, making it look casual yet perfect at the same time.

"I think I might ask Andrew to the winter formal," she announced. She watched for my reaction. I knew she'd had a crush on Andrew Fuller since ninth grade. Andrew was the president of the drama club, and Amanda was the vice president. The two of them were always at odds about the direction in which the club should move. They spent most of their time bickering, but it always seemed somewhat flirtatious. Andrew was one of the few people who never backed down from Amanda in an argument. I think that's why she liked him so much.

"You're going to ask him?" I couldn't fathom being so bold. Though, if any girl could pull off asking a guy to be her date to a dance, it was certainly Amanda.

"Sure, why not?" she said, pulling the elastic out of her hair and redoing her bun. This was Amanda's tell. When Amanda was feeling self-conscious, though she'd never admit it, she fidgeted endlessly with her hair. "I want to go with him; why shouldn't I ask him?"

"I guess," I said, though I still couldn't wrap my mind around the logic.

"Exactly!" Amanda clapped her hands as if the issue was settled, though I could have sworn I could still see the shadow of a doubt lingering in her smile. She jumped to her feet and scooped her phone off the bed. She hunched over the screen, her thumbs working wildly. When she was done, she turned the screen so I could see the lengthy blue bubble on her side of a conversation.

"Done," she proclaimed, dropping the device back down onto the bed.

"Seriously? Just like that?" I blinked at her. She never ceased to amaze me. She smiled widely.

"And now we wait."

As we both stared at her phone, I realized I was as nervous about the answer as she was. I knew Amanda was not nearly as confident as she liked to appear. If Andrew responded negatively, it would crush her. I watched Amanda redo her bun for the third time, and I remembered how devastated she was the last time she was passed over for a big part. I needed to drag her out of her bed. I didn't want to see the devastated Amanda, especially so close to the holidays. Though deep down, I was also a little nervous about what would happen if Andrew said yes.

I assumed that, just like we had for the past two years, Amanda and I would go to the Winter Formal together. If Amanda got a date, what would that mean for me? I shook the thoughts from my head, realizing how selfish they were. I was mentally scolding myself when the phone on the bed made a quiet ping.

Amanda and I looked at each other before she dove for the bed. She spun the phone around and took a deep breath before unlocking the screen. Unable to see the screen from where I was sitting on the floor, I watched Amanda's face. There was a moment of hesitation while her eyes moved across the line of text, and then I watched as they became wide pools of sparkling blue.

"Holy shit, he said yes!"

In obligatory best-friend fashion, I jumped to my feet and threw my hands in the air. We jumped around in celebration, as if we had just won some sort of joint prize. Secretly, I was aware I was actually celebrating my own loss. While Amanda was going to have a night to remember, it was likely that now I wouldn't attend the formal at all.

Like I said, you don't have to tell me how selfish that sounds. I'm totally aware even thinking those types of thoughts makes me a shitty best friend. At this point, you can just add it to the list of shitty things I've done to Amanda. I swear I wanted to be happy for her, and I was happy that Andrew said yes. I was just also aware of the consequences for me. The last two winter formals with Amanda had been so much fun; I was just disappointed things were going to be different this year.

As if she could hear my thoughts, Amanda sat down on the bed. She ran a hand down her face and crossed her legs, settling herself into seriousness.

"Now we need to find a date for you."

CHAPTER NINE

After Andrew agreed to go to the winter formal with her, Amanda became completely obsessed with the event. She convinced her mother to drive us to the mall three times that week so we could dress shop. Although not quite as formal as the title implied, the dance still required a cocktail-type dress. Amanda had always been an obsessive shopper, but now she was relentless, scouring the racks for the perfect dress.

In each store we visited, Amanda tried on six or seven dresses to every one I tried on. I shopped halfheartedly. Despite Amanda being adamant that she would find me a date, I was still pretty sure I would be staying home on the night of the formal. I'd come to the conclusion I wouldn't bother buying a new dress, and if, at the last minute, I did decide to go, I could just wear the dress from last year.

Amanda finished our third shopping trip empty-handed and was already planning to return to the mall the following day. When she asked me what time she should pick me up, I shook my head.

"I can't shop tomorrow. I'm having dinner with Grandma June."

Amanda pouted.

"Bring Grandma June! She's great with fashion."

"Amanda, I'm not dragging Grandma June to the mall to shop for winter formal dresses for you; she's too old for that."

"She's only sixty-five! That's like a spring chicken! She's still young enough to be having sex!"

I wrinkled my nose and smacked Amanda with my purse.

"Gross! Grandma June is not having sex!" My grandfather died of cancer before I was old enough to remember him. My grandmother had been the strong, single, female role model in my life ever since. Although I realized that Grandma June was not nearly as old as some of my other classmate's grandparents, certainly her grandmother status made her too old for dating and sex.

"All I'm saying is I hope I'm still getting some if I look like your grandma when I'm sixty-five!"

Although Amanda had never gotten any, she had recently become obsessed with the idea. We'd already discussed whether or not it would make her a slut if she decided Andrew could be her first after the winter formal. I think that's why she obsessed over her dress purchase. She planned on it being the dress she lost her virginity in.

I was still trying to force the idea of my grandmother having sex out of my head when Mrs. Attwood pulled up to the curb outside the mall.

"Still no bags, I see," she said as I slid into the backseat. Amanda collapsed into the front seat, letting out an exasperated sigh.

"I'm at a total loss, Mother." She threw her hands up dramatically. I watched Mrs. Attwood smile in the rearview mirror as she pulled the car back into evening traffic. I wondered if Mrs. Attwood suspected the real plans in store for Amanda's winter formal dress.

"You'll find something wonderful, I'm sure," she said. I'd echoed that sentiment dozens of times since we started shopping for this dress, but the words didn't appease Amanda.

Mrs. Attwood dropped me off in front of my house, and I waved as the car disappeared around the corner. Mrs. Attwood was so different from my own mother. I couldn't imagine my mother telling me I would find the perfect dress. The only advice my mother had offered me when I was shopping for my winter formal dress last year was that it absolutely needed to be black.

"Any other color will either clash with your hair or make you stand out like a sore thumb. A girl like you can't go wrong with black. It's simple and understated." I always wondered what my mother was envisioning when she said "a girl like you." Did she really think there were other girls like me out there, or was she just trying to soften the blows about me specifically?

When I came home with a simple black dress that was made of soft fabric and hung loosely around my legs, my mother frowned.

"It's a little frumpy, don't you think?" My shoulders slumped, and I hugged my arms around my waist.

"Amanda said it made me look tall and thin."

"Well, Amanda would say that, I guess." With that, my mother disappeared into her bedroom. I heard her open her own closet doors, and I imagined her standing in front of the array of cocktail dresses she'd collected over the years.

My mother would tell anyone who would listen that she was still the same dress size she had worn in high school. She even still had the dress she'd been wearing when she won the Homecoming Queen title the first time. Once, when I was younger, I asked her about the dress she'd been wearing when she won the title the second time. She smiled slyly and told me it had been ripped in the excitement of the night. I didn't know what that meant at the time, but I have a feeling I know what it means now.

It's not that I'm jealous of my mother. Don't write that down. I know she's gorgeous and she's always been gorgeous. She drove all the boys crazy in high school. In fact, she still does.

My mother goes on dates with men the same way some people go through library books. She checks them out just long enough to get a good read on them and then she sends them on their way.

Amanda refers to her as a serial dater. When she's finished with her prey, she rarely offers an explanation for the breakup. She just says they weren't compatible. I have no idea how it could be possible that there are so many men in the world that my mother isn't compatible with.

Statistics alone seem to suggest that at this point she should have found at least one man that could work. But statistics don't seem to apply to my mother, and every few weeks she finds a new victim to toy with for a few dates.

I know, I know, you're not here to analyze my mother and her relationships. We're here to talk about mine. I never imagined the winter formal would be the turning point of my junior year or my entire life. No one could have predicted that. It was supposed to be Amanda's night, but I guess it sort of turned into mine, instead.

I bet Amanda didn't see that coming, I know I didn't.

CHAPTER TEN

The winter formal is always held on the Friday before Christmas break. On the Wednesday before the dance, Amanda's stress level was through the roof. She still hadn't found a dress, and her mother told her this was the last night she could drive us to the mall. It was basically do-or-die time.

I promised Amanda I would accompany her to the mall as soon as school let out. Although I loved my best friend, I was particularly dreading the final bell. I knew it would be our most hectic shopping trip to date.

I was particularly gloomy when I took my seat at the bench in chemistry class. It was the last chemistry class before break, and Mr. Carter promised us we could watch a Christmas-themed movie instead of having a lecture. Although most kids were thrilled with this idea, it felt like a complete waste of a class to me. I can watch Christmas movies at home on my own time. If I'm going to be in class, I might as well be getting something accomplished.

I kept my displeasure to myself when Mr. Carter made the announcement. I knew it would only make me look like more of a freak if I were upset we weren't doing work. I slid onto my stool and put my notebook in front of me, mostly out of habit. It was flipped to a clean page, and I figured maybe I could occupy myself by catching up on writing out some study guides while the rest of the class focused on the movie.

I was aware of the moment Adam slid onto the stool next to me, though I tried to remain unfazed by his presence. Try as I might, I couldn't help the slight flutter in my stomach as I caught the scent of him. It made me a little lightheaded as I recalled being surrounded by it for the entire afternoon I'd worn his sweatshirt.

Mr. Carter turned the lights off, and *Elf* filled the screen. It's a movie we've all seen a dozen times, but you can't help laughing at Will Ferrell. I was actually watching the movie when Adam pulled my notebook out from in front of me.

I raised an eyebrow as he slid my notebook across the desk until it was positioned in a way that he could write using his left hand. I don't know why I always found it so cute that he's left-handed. I watched as his hand moved across the page, what he was doing blocked from my view. When he finished, he slid the notebook back in front of me.

R u going to the dance on friday?

The words were cramped into the upper corner of the blank page, as if he hadn't wanted to use up too much space in my notebook. I picked up my pen and considered my answer.

Probably, you?

He pulled the notebook back within his reach. When he returned it to where I could read it, I thought my heart might actually stop beating. I stared down at the words he had written under my own.

yup. want to go together?

I blinked and reached slowly for my pen, allowing myself ample time to read the words multiple times to ensure I was not mistaken. Was Adam Lincoln asking me to go to the winter formal with him?

Adam Lincoln.

The Adam Lincoln had just written me a note to ask me to go to the winter formal with him.

Sure.

I didn't want to sound too eager, though the phrase "are you fucking kidding me?" had crossed through my mind.

I waited.

I think I was holding my breath. As he pulled the notebook back in front of him, I suddenly expected him to burst out laughing. I had a flash of fear where I imagined everyone, even Mr. Carter, was in on this prank. I imagined Adam standing up and announcing that I'd fallen for his joke. I pictured the entire class turning to laugh at me instead of the movie. Maybe Mr. Carter would even pause the movie so everyone could truly enjoy the outcome of the prank. *How could you be so gullible, Sasha?* he would say.

But Adam pushed the notebook back in front of me, and the words were still there.

cool. gimme your number and ill text u.

I hastily scrawled my cell phone number on the page, and he pulled his phone out of his pocket. Under the lab table, I watched him type the number into his phone. A second later, I felt my own phone vibrate against my leg. I glanced down at it and saw the message on my screen.

hey its adam

I nodded and saved the contact into my phone. Adam smiled and slid his phone away and folded his arms across the desk. He casually rested his chin on his arms and laughed at the movie for the rest of the period. With his head turned that way, he couldn't see me staring at him, wondering what in the world had just happened.

Adam Lincoln had asked me to the winter formal.

I had a date to the winter formal.

That date was Adam Lincoln.

CHAPTER ELEVEN

I debated whether to even tell Amanda about Adam asking me to the dance. I know how that sounds, but I just knew she wouldn't be happy about it. I figured she'd go into some dramatic scenario where she'd claim he was setting me up. I just didn't want to hear it, mostly because I was already having those thoughts on my own and I didn't need to hear them from her, too.

It wasn't so hard to believe this was all part of some master plan to make a fool out of me. I wouldn't have necessarily been surprised if you told me Adam left chemistry class and went straight to fill in his baseball buddies. I could imagine them all standing together, doubled over in laughter as he relayed the way I had wholeheartedly fallen for his joke.

By the time I slide into the spot next to Amanda at the lunch table, my head was swimming with concerns about the possibilities of pranks and embarrassment. Would Adam just stand me up? Leave me waiting at the door for him to never arrive? Or would he pick me up and then plan some public embarrassment once we arrived? I was so consumed by my fears, I didn't notice anyone had spoken to me. Amanda and Andrew were both staring at me expectantly, clearly awaiting the answer to a question I hadn't heard.

"Uh, sorry. What?"

Amanda rolled her eyes.

"Andrew feels he should have some input on the color of my dress at this point so he can make sure he has a matching shirt." Although Amanda was acting annoyed, I could tell by her smirk she was loving this playful banter with Andrew.

"Of course I should!" Andrew banged his fist against the table like a gavel. "If she'd just picked out a dress weeks ago like every other girl in the school…" Andrew fluttered his hand through the air. Amanda laughed.

"What do you know about every other girl in the school?"

"Do you have a dress already?" Andrew pointed his yogurt spoon in my direction. I opened my mouth to answer, but Amanda cut me off.

"As a matter of fact, she does not. So there goes your theory!"

Andrew retorted, and he and Amanda lost themselves in bickering again. I turned my attention toward the sandwich in front of me, though already my mind was reverting to thoughts of Adam.

Maura Lawrence leaned in and bumped me with her elbow.

"What are your plans for the dance this year? Going with anyone?" Maura always struck me as a weird combination of Amanda and me. She was every bit the nerd that I was, though where I preferred sciences and math, Maura leaned toward history and current events. Most of the time she was quiet and kept to herself, but she was the captain of the debate club, and during a debate she was as loud and outgoing as Amanda was on stage. Maura's confidence in her opinions was unshakable, which unfortunately caused a lot of people who didn't know her well to label her as a know-it-all.

"Well, actually, I do think I'm going with someone." I glanced at

Amanda, who must have thought my look was a plea for help. She draped her arm over my shoulders and pulled me against her.

"Of course she is," Amanda said to Maura over the top of my head. "She's coming with Andrew and me, right, Andrew?" Andrew's eyes were wide. This was clearly the first time he had heard of this plan, and having a third wheel was apparently not what he'd envisioned for the night. He was attempting to stammer out a response when I shook free of Amanda's grasp.

"No," I said, a little more firmly than I intended. "Someone asked me. Someone else asked me."

Amanda stared at me. I couldn't tell if she was shocked by my statement or hurt that I hadn't told her already.

"It only just happened," I said to her quickly, by way of an apology.

"Oh, oh, who is it?" Maura asked. She leaned in closer, as if I were about to share a secret.

"Um, Adam. Adam Lincoln."

Maura squealed at the name and Amanda's eyes went wide. No one else was paying attention. Andrew apparently didn't care who I was attending the dance with as long as it wasn't with him.

"Oh my God! You are so lucky!" Maura bobbed up and down in her seat and clapped her hands together. "I'm so jealous. How did it happen? Tell me everything."

Amanda was nodding, though I couldn't quite read her expression.

"He's my lab partner in chem class. Today while we were watching Elf, he wrote me a note."

"A note?" Amanda raised an eyebrow, and the doubt in her tone was unmistakable.

Maura squealed again.

"That is so cute!"

"Yeah, a note." I opened my notebook up on the table, and Maura and Amanda both leaned in to look.

I was almost surprised to see the note was still there. Part of me was convinced I could have imagined the whole thing. But there it was, plain as day for Amanda and Maura to read. My loopy handwriting slanting in one direction and his scratchy letters slanting in the other.

"Well, would you look at that." Amanda leaned back and took a bite of her egg salad. "You're going to the winter formal with Adam Lincoln."

"I guess I am," I said, daring to allow myself to believe it was true.

"Looks like you'll need to buy a dress tonight after all."

CHAPTER TWELVE

Amanda didn't lecture me about pranks like I expected her to. In fact, she didn't say anything negative at all about Adam taking me to the dance. On the ride to the mall, she criticized her mother for driving too slowly.

"We need to get there ASAP, Mother."

"The mall is not going anywhere, Amanda Marie."

"You can't possibly understand how important today's mission is, Mom. We have so much to do and simply not enough time to do it."

"I'm sure you'll be fine." Mrs. Attwood pulled the car to the curb in front of the mall's front entrance. "I'll pick you girls up at six o'clock sharp. Sasha, sweetheart, don't let her run you ragged." She smiled at me as I closed the door. Amanda didn't wait for her mother to drive away before grabbing my hand and pulling me into the mall.

"I know we did Macy's already, but let's go back. I think I want to look at that pink dress again. Something tells me that's the one Andrew is going to like the best."

Amanda dragged me across the mall and through the double doors of Macy's. She beelined for the section we'd spent nearly two hours in on the first day of this endeavor. She disappeared into a rack of dresses and emerged a few minutes later with a pink dress I vaguely remembered her refusing to try on during our first trip.

I followed her to the dressing room, where she slipped inside one of the stalls. She was talking to herself from behind the door, mumbling about the fact that she should have skipped dessert last night.

When she opened the door, she was wearing a look I instantly recognized. She was self-conscious. I saw it in her face as she awkwardly smoothed the fabric across her waist.

Amanda Attwood was almost never self-conscious. She had no problem standing on a stage in front of a crowd of people wearing various costumes. She could sing her heart out or recite line after line of dialog without ever feeling stage fright. She was my fearless best friend. But in this moment, she looked a lot more like me than herself.

In reality, Amanda had no reason to be self-conscious. The dress looked amazing on her. It hugged her body just enough to accentuate her hourglass shape. The color was perfect for her skin tone. She was glowing. It was cut just deep enough in the front to show off the cleavage Amanda was most proud of. It was the perfect dress. Why hadn't she selected this one in the first place?

"That's the dress," I said as firmly as I could. I wanted to reassure her the way she had done for me on countless occasions.

"Do you think so?" Amanda turned back towards the mirror, smoothing the fabric and adjusting the straps on her shoulders. She twisted a lock of her hair around her finger as she eyed her reflection.

"One hundred percent, without a doubt." I watched her fidget with the material, though She was standing a little straighter than when she'd first come out of the dressing room. "Andrew is going to love it."

With that, Amanda broke into a smile. She twirled around a few times in the mirror, admiring the dress from all angles. Finally satisfied, she declared she was going to need new shoes as well. She closed the door of the dressing room to change out of the dress.

"So," she said through the door, "Adam Lincoln, huh?"

"Yeah." I was glad the door was between us so I didn't have to look her in the eyes. There was silence for a minute.

"You're going to need a way better dress than last year to impress Adam Lincoln."

I realized I'd been holding my breath and let it out in a laugh.

"Well, I guess now that we've got yours out of the way, we can focus on me."

Amanda threw the door of her dressing room open, the pink dress draped over her arm. "I know just the one!"

Before I knew it, we were back in the same dressing room, though this time the roles were reversed. Amanda was rambling on the other side of the door about whether she should have Andrew wear a white or black shirt. She presented it like she was asking my opinion, but I knew better than to bother trying to answer her. I listened to her carry on with herself while I changed into the dress she'd selected for me. I opened the stall door without bother to check the mirror. I knew Amanda's opinion of the dress would matter more than mine anyway.

Amanda was facing away from my dressing room, flipping through the hangers on the returns rack when I opened the door. She spun toward me, mid-sentence in her debate between black and white. When she saw me, her eyes widened and her jaw dropped. It might have been the first time Amanda Attwood had ever been speechless.

"Holy shit."

"Is it that bad?" I looked down at the navy-blue fabric.

"Are you kidding me? Did you not look at yourself?"

Amanda grabbed my arm and pulled me out of the tiny dressing stall until I was standing in front of the large, 180-degree mirror at the end of the dressing room. I examined myself in the mirror, and what I saw shocked me.

The dress was simple, a scoop neck top with three-quarter-length sleeves, but it hugged my body all the way down my thighs. It was shorter than anything I'd ever worn before, but the length made my legs look long.

"That's the one." Amanda was standing behind me, her arms crossed in front of her chest. She nodded, almost as if to say the decision was made. She glanced up at the wall clock. "Which is perfect; we have just enough time to go find shoes."

One hundred and ten dollars later, I carried my Macy's purchases towards Mrs. Attwood's car. I felt a little guilty about spending so much on a dress I was probably only going to wear once, but Amanda argued that since I only spent twenty dollars on last year's dress, so I deserved to spend a bit more on this one.

She was exaggerating, obviously. But compared to the two-hundred-dollar dress she had purchased last year, my thirty-five-dollar dress had been very inexpensive.

"Besides," she said, as the cashier handed me the receipt for my purchases, "you didn't go to the formal with Adam Lincoln last year."

I was sitting in the back of Mrs. Attwood's Toyota when my phone vibrated. I pulled it out of my pocket and read the message on the screen.

my dad said i could borrow the car for friday. pick u up at 6:30?

This was really happening. I was really going to the winter formal as Adam Lincoln's date.

Sounds good to me.

Adam responded with the thumbs-up emoji. I floated into the house after Mrs. Attwood dropped me off.

CHAPTER THIRTEEN

Is it weird that I tried not to let myself get too excited about the dance over the next two days? I kept telling myself this could all still be a sick prank. I managed to avoid telling my mother Adam was supposed to be picking me up, just in case he never did. My plan was to get dressed for the dance in my room, and if Adam didn't show up, I'd simply come out and tell my mother I wasn't feeling well and decided to stay home.

I'm sure you never worried about being stood up, looking like that. I imagine the boys were lining up at the door to take you to dances. Or maybe you were one of those popular girls that declared themselves as "having too much fun being single to be tied down." We've got a group of girls like that at school, too. They're all gorgeous and they know all the boys want them. They go to dances as a group and stand in a circle grinding on each other to make the boys jealous. At the end of the night, you can find every single one of them under the bleachers with someone's tongue down their throat. Apparently, that's the fun part of being single that I was missing.

In case Adam really did show up, I went with Amanda to get my hair done. Amanda had her hair pinned in an up-do. I watched as the lady used bobby pin after bobby pin to place each piece of Amanda's hair with precision. When she was done, she coated the whole thing with so much hair spray, I imagined that Amanda's hair would stay like that for a week.

When it was my turn, the hairdresser spun me away from the mirror and asked me what I wanted.

"I was hoping for something kind of natural. Down. Just not so…frizzy." The woman examined my hair and nodded knowingly. She set to work using different mists of sprays and flat irons and curlers. When she spun me back toward the mirror, I couldn't believe I was even looking at my own hair.

Although still quite obviously red, it was sleek and smooth and falling in bouncing ringlets around my shoulders. I reached up to touch it, but stopped myself, afraid I was going to mess it up. After we paid, I walked to the car stiffly, trying not to move too much. Amanda laughed and told me that if I walked like that, people were going to think I had a stick up my ass.

Two hours later, I was standing in front of the mirror on my closet door. I wore my new dress and the strappy tan heels Amanda had picked out for me. My hair still looked as good as when we'd left the salon, and I delicately applied mascara to my eyelashes. I was really hoping Adam Lincoln actually showed up, because I was pretty sure that for once, I actually looked good.

I glanced at the time and peered out the window. I didn't want it to be obvious I was watching for him, but I wanted to make sure I saw his car before my mother did. At a quarter of seven, I was getting nervous. Maybe this was a scam, after all. I should have known that Adam was never going to take me to the dance. I was cursing myself for being so stupid when the headlights pulled up to the front of the house.

I wanted to run to the door, but I wasn't used to walking in four-inch heels. My mother got there just as I was rounding the corner. She didn't bother to hide her surprise when she opened it either.

"Adam? How nice to see you again. What are you doing here?"

"I'm here to pick up Sasha. Sorry I'm late. It's harder than it looks to tie this tie."

My mother stepped back to let Adam through the door.

"Pick up Sasha? Well, come in, I…"

I don't know what my mother was going to say, because at that exact moment, she and Adam both saw me. I was standing in the kitchen doorway, shifting my weight from one heel to the other. My mother's jaw couldn't have dropped any lower. She stammered something, but I didn't bother to try to hear it. Adam was smiling at me. I met his eyes, and he stepped forward.

"This is for you." He handed me a red rose wrapped in tissue paper. I wasn't sure what I was supposed to do with it. Was I supposed to put it in water here or take it with me? I felt stupid asking. I held on to it awkwardly until my mother swooped forward and took it from me.

"I'll put this in water," she said, shooing us toward the door. "You two go have fun." She waved to us from the doorway as we drove away in Adam's dad's car. Adam apologized again for being late. I told him it was fine.

"I hope you didn't think I wasn't coming."

My eyes widened, and I wondered if he knew that was exactly what I'd been thinking as the minutes ticked by before he arrived. He laughed and turned the music up.

As the school got closer, I panicked. I was sure this was all a mistake, certain I had set myself up to be embarrassed. But what could I do now? I was already in the car. It was too chilly to tell Adam to let me out on the side of the road without a coat, and I would never have been able to walk all the way home in those heels. The only thing to do was show up at the dance and accept my fate. When worst came to worst, I would just have to find Amanda and

Andrew and hope they would take me home.

By the time Adam parked the car outside of the gym, I was nearly hyperventilating.

"You okay?" Adam watched me, the concern evident on his face. I took a deep breath, trying to calm my nerves.

"Listen," I whispered, staring down at my strappy shoes, "if this is all part of some prank, I'd rather just go home now...."

The tears were welling uncontrollably in my eyes. I fought to keep them from falling, telling myself it was because I didn't want to ruin my makeup. Adam reached across the car and rested his hand on my bare knee. The warmth seemed to radiate up my leg.

"Do you really think I'm the type of guy who would ask you out as a prank?"

I couldn't bring myself to look at him, but I could feel his eyes on the side of my face. I shook my head and shrugged. I was still fighting the tears and didn't trust myself to speak.

"Come on, Sash." Adam gently squeezed my knee. I flicked my eyes in his direction and he smiled. "I like you. I asked you to the dance because I think we have some real chemistry." I couldn't help but laugh at his corny joke. A tear escaped, but Adam wiped it away with his thumb. "All jokes aside, I asked you to the dance because I want to go to the dance with you. Will you go inside with me?"

I nodded, and Adam smiled so wide his dimples looked like canyons. He squeezed my knee again before opening his door and climbing out. I took a deep breath and did the same. Adam offered me his elbow. I looped my arm through his, and we walked toward the gymnasium doors together.

CHAPTER FOURTEEN

On that Friday night in December, I would have never guessed things would end like this.

I walked into the gym still riding the high of being on Adam Lincoln's arm. I pushed the doubts into the back of my mind. I was there because he liked me. I was finally letting myself believe this wasn't a prank.

The gym had been decorated by the student counsel with some cheap, snowflake-themed cardboard cutouts. There were white Christmas lights strung between the sections of bleachers and some streamers hanging from the basketball hoops. It was tacky and tasteless, but no one seemed to mind.

Inside the gym, the lights were off and the DJ was playing music much louder than necessary to fill the space. The school-required chaperones were gathered in the hallway outside the gym, yelling over the noise and apparently trying to pretend they were anywhere other than a high school dance.

Adam led me inside, and no one doused me in pig's blood or silly string. I forced myself to relax as he led me over to a group of baseball players standing near one of the sections of bleachers. The boys formed a circle around their girlfriends, who danced together in the center. It was like they had created a fence for their girlfriends to exist inside of. Adam took his place in the outside ring, and I toed the gym floor nervously, unsure of what I was supposed to do next.

After what felt like an eternity of social discomfort, one of the girls inside the circle seemed to notice me. She took my hand and pulled me toward her. We spun around the circle and bounced off the other girls inside the ring. We jumped up and down in time with the music, and it wasn't long before I understood why they were all barefoot. I kicked my shoes into the pile that had formed just outside of the ring of baseball players and continued to dance with the other girls.

When the music slowed, all the girls immediately found their respective partners and draped themselves around them. I found Adam in the circle, and he put his hands gently on my hips. I glanced around, aware that some people were watching us. He urged me closer to him with his hands, moving them from my hips onto the tops of my ass cheeks. We swayed back and forth together to the music. When the song was over, he leaned in and asked if I was having fun. He smiled when I nodded, and he pushed me back toward the other girls, who resumed jumping up and down in the center of the circle.

"I'm going to go try to find Amanda," I yelled over the thumping bass. Adam frowned.

"Stay here with me."

"I'll just be gone a minute. I just want to say hi."

Adam looked disappointed. He held my hand as I walked away, holding onto my fingers until I had to pull them free of his grasp. I hurried around the outside of the dance floor, peering into the groups of bouncing bodies, looking for Amanda. She loved to dance. I was certain I would find her among a circle of other drama stars who were twirling around, screaming the words to the song into make-believe microphones. But as I scanned the groups of sweaty bodies, I couldn't find her. On my second pass around the gym, Adam grabbed my hand and pulled me back toward him.

"You've been gone for forever."

"I still haven't found Amanda."

"But you found me." Adam grinned at me as he pulled me against him. As if on cue, the music slowed. I looped my arms around his neck and allowed him to hold us together.

As the love song droned on, he leaned in and pressed his lips against mine. I tried not to act surprised. His tongue slipped between my lips and forced its way into my mouth. His breath tasted like cinnamon and something else I couldn't quite place. I felt dizzy with emotion as he slid his fingers into my hair. I sank into his kiss, allowing it to wash over me. I don't even know how long we stood there.

After what felt like forever and not long enough all at the same time, Adam broke away from me. He ran a sleeve across his mouth and winked at me. I suddenly felt unsteady on my feet without his body supporting me. One of his friends punched him in the arm, and I realized his teammates and their girlfriends had all been watching.

One of the girls, I don't even know which one, reached for me and pulled me back into the group to continue to dance. She smiled at me knowingly as we jumped around. The rest of the night continued just like that. We would jump and twirl until the music slowed, at which point Adam would pull me close and kiss me deeply. When the DJ announced the last song, Adam seemed to hold me even tighter. This time, before he kissed me, he leaned in to whisper into my ear.

"I told you I liked you."

I knew I was blushing; I just hoped it wasn't noticeable in the dim light.

"I like you, too."

"Will you be my girlfriend?"

I pulled back slightly, looking him in the eye. I was sure I must have misheard him. I couldn't believe, even after the night we'd just had, that Adam Lincoln would want me to be his girlfriend. But he was watching me expectantly, waiting for me to answer. I nodded, unable to think of a verbal response that seemed to fit the situation.

He pulled me against him again and kissed me, sealing the deal. I kissed him back, my mind screaming inside my head.

I was kissing Adam Lincoln, who was now my boyfriend.

Somebody pinch me.

CHAPTER FIFTEEN

The ride home was a complete blur. I was staring at our hands interlaced together on the center console, trying to figure out how I managed to get to this point. How did I, Sasha Collins, the nerdy girl with unruly hair and no social skills to speak of, become Adam Lincoln's girlfriend in one night?

If you're wondering if I had any doubt in those initial moments, if there was even the slightest hint about what was to come, the answer is no. I would never have imagined that less than a year later, you and I would be sitting here talking about how it all went so horribly wrong. But in fairness, does anyone really spend those first blissful minutes of a relationship thinking about how it all might go down in flames?

As soon as we pulled up in front of my house, Adam leaned across the seat and pressed his lips against mine again. His tongue was forceful, almost desperate, as if he were trying to find his way deeper into my mouth. I wasn't totally sure what I was supposed to do in return. I bent one of my arms awkwardly so it sort of rested on Adam's shoulder, but the way we were positioned, him leaning across the center console and me still buckled into the passenger seat, there wasn't much more I could manage.

After what felt like twenty minutes but was probably only a minute or two, Adam pulled back, a goofy smile plastered on his face. His cheeks were flushed pink, and he had the look of someone who'd just gotten off their favorite amusement park ride. It made me feel a little silly, too.

We sat in silence, and then I realized my mother was more than likely watching us from the front window. The realization made me a little panicky. I unlatched my seatbelt and went to open the door.

"Wait!" Adam said, grabbing my arm to prevent me from climbing out of the car. I watched as he pulled off the class ring he was wearing. He held it out to me.

"You're my girlfriend now," he said, and my heart skipped at the reminder. "You have to wear this now for me."

I took the ring from him and slipped it onto my ring finger. The heavy gold ring was engraved with Adam's initials and his baseball number. It was several sizes too big for my finger, and I felt the heavy face of it immediately spin toward my palm. I clenched my fist tightly so the ring wouldn't slip off my hand.

I gave Adam another kiss before telling him I really had to go inside. Disappointment flashed in his eyes, but he smiled widely when I agreed to see him the following day.

When I reached the front door, I turned back to the street, half-expecting this to be the point where I woke up from a dream. I was still convinced there was no way this could be my reality. But Adam was still parked out on the street, the interior light on inside the car so I could see him beaming as he watched me walk up the path. I gave a little wave and then slipped through the door.

Once inside, I leaned back against the door and took a deep breath. I hugged my arms around myself, trying to slow my heartbeat. I unbuckled my shoes and carried them down the hallway toward the kitchen. My mother was seated at the kitchen table with a mug of green tea in front of her. She looked almost as giddy as I felt as she raised the mug to her lips.

"Have fun?" she asked, wagging her eyebrows in a ridiculous way. I nodded as I sank down into the chair opposite her, dropping my shoes onto the tile floor. I could tell from the way that she was looking at me over the rim of her cup that she had been watching us when we pulled up out front. She probably slipped back into the kitchen when I started making my way to the front door. "Adam is a handsome boy."

"He asked me to be his girlfriend." I whispered the words, as if saying them too loudly might break the spell. My mother clapped her hands in front of her and let out a high-pitched squeal of excitement. She looked prouder in that moment than I'd ever seen her.

She began rapidly firing off questions about how the night had played out. She wanted to know everything, like we were two best friends gossiping in the backseat of the school bus. She didn't even wait for one question to be fully answered before she launched into her next.

As my mother bombarded me with questions, I felt my body start to relax. As I replayed the night for her, the events started to feel more real to me. I became more confident that I hadn't imagined that first deep kiss on the dance floor or the way Adam looked at me as he waited for me to tell him whether or not I would be his girlfriend. My mother was ecstatic as I shared the details with her.

"You're a lucky girl," she kept saying as I told her about Adam pulling me against him for each slow song. When I showed her Adam's ring, she put a hand on her chest and remarked at how "wonderfully traditional" Adam was.

"It's too big," I said, spinning the ring easily around my knuckle. "I'm afraid I'm going to lose it."

My mother rolled her eyes in pretend exasperation.

"You're not going to wear it on your hand, silly," she said, pushing away from the table. She disappeared down the hall and returned a moment later with a gold chain. She slipped the ring onto the chain and fastened it around my neck.

"See?" she said as she sat back down across from me. She launched back into her inquiry into the night's events. I fingered Adam's ring dangling around my neck as I answered her questions in vivid detail.

After I relayed the whole night to her at least two separate times, my mother finally pushed away from the table and placed her mug in the sink. She kissed my forehead on the way out of the kitchen, leaving me alone while my mind and body buzzed with excitement.

I wasn't ready to be done talking about the whole magical night, I decided. I raced down the hall to my room and found my cell phone where I'd left it plugged into the charger. Glancing at the digital clock next to my bed, I decided quarter to midnight was not too late to call my best friend. Surely, she would still be up. She and Andrew planned to go out after the dance. Well, actually, she and Andrew planned to have sex after the dance. I figured an hour and a half was probably more than enough time to have accomplished that.

I waited for my phone to power on, but before I had the chance to click on Amanda's contact to call her, my phone started vibrating with incoming notifications. Amanda had called and texted me repeatedly, starting not long after the dance had started.

Are you here yet?

Where are you?

Helllllllo?

Seriously where are you?

No for real. I need you

Andrew is being a total dick

Why aren't you answering me?

Whatever. I'm going home

I scrolled through the messages, guilt suddenly gripping my stomach. I'd been so wrapped up in my own magical night, I totally forgot about Amanda. After I couldn't find her the first time, I never looked for her again.

I glanced at the time again and typed out a hasty reply.

I'm so sorry. I didn't bring my phone. I looked for you but couldn't find you. What happened?

I added a little heart shaped emoji before hitting send. I felt like the worst friend in the world. I had figured I wouldn't need my cell phone at the dance, since anyone I would have texted was also going to be there. I'd left it at home rather than risk losing it because I had nowhere to keep it.

I should have tried harder to find Amanda. I should have spent more time looking. I shouldn't have spent all night with Adam and his friends. But there was nothing I could do now to change it. I waited for Amanda to reply to my message, but as the minutes ticked by, I realized she hadn't even read it yet. Maybe she had gone to bed early. This sent a new pang of guilt through me. She went to bed mad with no one to talk to. I truly was the worst best friend.

I started and deleted several more messages to Amanda, but I just couldn't find the words to express how sorry I was. The guilt started to suck the excitement out of my night. I was no longer wrapped in the dreamy sensation of how wonderful the whole night had been.

At ten after midnight, I gave up on getting a response from Amanda. I put my phone down on the bedside table and was climbing under the covers when I heard the vibration. I grabbed the phone, prepared to renew my efforts of trying to word an apology. But the name on the screen wasn't Amanda. It was Adam.

goodnight beautiful. see u tomorrow.

I stared at the words glowing from the screen of my phone. I reread them over and over, letting the warm sensation flood through me again. I knew I should feel guilty. I knew I was still a terrible friend. But I couldn't pretend the sight of those words didn't make me feel better.

I put the phone down and slipped off to sleep, feeling as happy as I had when I'd first gotten home.

CHAPTER SIXTEEN

I woke up to my phone ringing, the vibration sounding like a jackhammer against the top of my nightstand. I groped for the phone and put it to my ear without opening my eyes to check the screen. My voice was thick with sleep I didn't try to hide as I said hello.

"Good morning, sleepy head!" I bolted upright at the sound of Adam's voice. Instinctively, my hand went to my hair, as if he might be able to tell how messy it was through the phone. I cleared my throat and glanced at the clock. It was just before ten.

"Good morning," I stammered, the events from last night flooding back to me. Adam was calling me first thing in the morning. I was Adam's girlfriend. I had a panicky thought that maybe Adam was calling to end the whole thing. He had time to think about it overnight and decided it was all a bad idea. It was better to just end it now and pretend like it never happened. I settled back against my pillow, trying to calm myself.

"Do you still want to hang out today?"

"Sure," I said, though even as I said it, I wondered if that seemed too desperate. Was I still supposed to be playing hard to get? I had no idea how this worked.

"Perfect. I'll pick you up in an hour. See you then"

"An hour?" I asked, but the line was dead before the words even left my mouth.

I looked at the phone's screen to confirm the call was no longer connected. In doing so, I saw I had missed several text messages while I was asleep.

The first two were from Adam, asking if I was up. I guess he decided against waiting for me to reply.

The last message was from Amanda. The sting of guilt hit me again as I read the message.

Last night was a disaster.

I asked her what happened, figuring now was not the time to mention that I thought last night was magical.

Andrew is such a jerk. He started flirting with Brittany right in front of me, like, for real, and when I called him out on it, he told me I couldn't stop him because we weren't a thing yet. Then he danced with her. THEN he had the nerve to ask me if we were still going out after the dance. Can you even?!

What a dick.

I knew Amanda was in one of her moods. She wouldn't require much response from me in order to stay on her rant. She was only looking for support. She sent several more messages about how Brittany was also at fault, as Brittany was fully aware Amanda and Andrew were going to the dance together. Amanda assumed Brittany was jealous and had purposely tried to ruin things between them. I supported Amanda during the pauses in her rant, all while rushing around to get ready for Adam to pick me up.

Want to binge Chinese food and watch Christmas movies?

I responded that I couldn't. I knew it was inevitable that Amanda would ask why not, but part of me still hoped this would be the one time Amanda just took me at my word. I didn't want to have to tell her I was going out with Adam, because that would turn the conversation towards how wonderful my night had been.

But just as I expected, Amanda asked me why. She even accompanied the message with several pouting emoji faces.

I started to type my response but erased it and restarted it several times. Finally, I decided to just lay it all out there for her, knowing if I didn't, there would just be more follow-up questions.

I'm going out with Adam. He asked me to be his girlfriend last night and I said yes and when he was dropping me off he asked me if I wanted to hang out today and I didn't know what to say so I said yes and now he's picking me up in 15 minutes.

I watched the three little dots appear and disappear on Amanda's end. When her message finally came through, all it said was **wow**. Just that one word. I didn't know how to read that. Was it a wow like she can't believe that happened or a wow like she doesn't know what to say? With Amanda, it honestly could have been anything.

I waited another minute to see if she said anything else before I added a simple **I'm sorry**.

Oh, you don't have to be sorry. Text me when you get home.

I was a little surprised Amanda hadn't seemed happier for me. I know her night had gone badly, but I'd assumed that when I finally got around to telling her my good news, she would be able to celebrate with me. I was still trying to figure this out when I heard a honk outside.

I raced down the stairs and checked the front window. Adam's rusty pickup truck was parked out front. Though not as nice-looking as the car he'd borrowed for the dance, the truck seemed to suit him better. As I climbed inside, Adam watched me excitedly. As soon as I was settled in the seat, he leaned over and placed a kiss on my lips.

"Hi there, girlfriend!"

I knew my cheeks were turning red, but I hardly had time to give in to the embarrassment before Adam gunned the engine in the old truck and we took off down the road.

We parked at the mall, which was unsurprisingly packed with last-minute Christmas shoppers. Adam grabbed my hand as we plunged into the throngs of people trying to find the perfect gift the day before the big day. Adam led me through the shoppers toward Yankee Candle, where we sniffed expensive candles in jars. Adam purchased my favorite one to give to his mom. We then wandered a few department stores looking for something for his dad. After that, we headed to the food court.

Adam ordered a basket of chicken fingers, and I ordered a slice of pizza. We sat together in the corner of the crowded food court, listening to the buzz of the shoppers around us nearly drown out the continuous loop of Christmas carols.

"My mom wants you to come over tomorrow night. We do the whole Christmas Eve dinner thing. With all the fish. You like fish, right?"

"Uh, yeah, but tomorrow is Christmas Eve."

"I know, that's usually when most people do Christmas Eve dinner."

I blushed, feeling stupid.

"I meant, like, you want me to meet your family on Christmas Eve?"

"Of course I do. Say you'll come. Please?"

I watched the woman at the next table try to entice a toddler to eat her chicken nuggets. The toddler looked like she was one refusal away from a full-blown meltdown.

I imagined what it would be like to spend Christmas Eve at my boyfriend's house with all his family. I'd spent every Christmas Eve for the last eight years at Amanda's house. I knew their traditions like the back of my hand. They always had ham on Christmas Eve, and we would stuff ourselves before moving on to dessert no one had room for but everyone ate. After dessert, we would do the Elephant Swap, where everyone brought a ridiculous gift and exchanged them like they were precious medals. After that, there was always caroling that ended in tears of laughter before everyone headed to bed in anticipation of Christmas morning.

A part of me couldn't imagine not spending Christmas Eve with the Attwoods. But the other part of me rationalized this was part of growing up. At some point, I would have my own life with my own Christmas traditions that didn't revolve around the Attwoods. Maybe this was how that transition started.

Adam had his hands clasped in a make-believe prayer and was repeating the word "please" over and over. He looked so childish, it was hard to believe that the boy sitting across from me was the same guy who confidently strutted through the halls of Baymont High.

"Okay, I'll be there," I said while trying to tell myself that Amanda would understand. Adam leapt from his chair and wrapped me in a hug.

"It'll be great," he promised into my ear before planting another solid kiss against my lips. I basked in this public display of affection. Amanda always scoffed at couples like this. When we would go to the mall together, she would wrinkle her nose and loudly make comments about couples kissing this way. "Get a room," she would say as she shuffled past them. While I always nodded in agreement, it didn't actually bother me nearly as much as they seemed to bother Amanda.

I was usually more jealous of the couple than anything else. Imagine being so in love with someone you don't care where you are or what's going on around you. As Adam's tongue danced around in my mouth, I couldn't help but wonder if there were people around us thinking the same thing. I wondered if someone else thought it looked like Adam loved me in that moment.

When we finally came up for air, I stole a look around us. The only person who seemed to notice us at all was the mother at the next table. Her toddler was now happily eating the cookie that came with her unfinished meal. The mother clicked her tongue, apparently sharing the same thoughts as Amanda. In the instant our eyes met, she shook her head disapprovingly.

Adam cleaned up our table, and we wandered through the mall for a while longer. Adam pointed out items in windows he thought I would look good in. When we reached Victoria's Secret, Adam whistled as he pointed to a mannequin wearing lacy lingerie.

"I bet you'd look hot in that," Adam exclaimed loudly as we passed the display. I tried to hide my embarrassment at the thought of wearing such an outfit, hoping no one around us had heard. I couldn't possibly wear such a sexy outfit, and the thought of wearing it in front of Adam was even more mortifying. Thankfully, Adam didn't linger in front of the window for long.

"I should get home," I told him, glancing at my watch. I saw the same flash of disappointment in Adam's eyes, but he nodded and led me toward the mall's exit. On the ride home, Adam provided me with an overview of what I could expect from Christmas Eve dinner.

It was apparently a formal affair and he encouraged me to dress up.

"Try and do your hair like it was last night," Adam said, looking at the unruly curls that had returned after my shower this morning. I self-consciously reached up to smooth my mane. "You looked really hot last night," he added.

I tried to remember the steps I had watched the hairdresser take in order to blow my curls straight. I imagined that Amanda would be able to replicate the look, but she would be busy with her own Christmas Eve preparations. The thought reminded me I was going to have to tell Amanda I didn't plan on spending Christmas Eve with her family.

After Adam dropped me off at home, I called Amanda. She answered on the second ring, the telltale sound of rustling tissue paper in the background.

"How was your date?" she asked, without even saying hello.

"Good, I think."

"You think?" I could hear the frown in her voice.

"It seems like Adam likes me."

"I would certainly hope so, since he asked you to be his girlfriend."

"Well, yeah, that would make sense."

My voice trailed off. This suddenly felt weird. There was an awkward silence, and I realized that in all the years Amanda and I had been talking on the phone, there had never been silence like this.

Usually, I was barely able to get a word in edgewise while Amanda filled the space with her chatter. I waited for Amanda to say something else, but all I heard was sound of scissors slicing through wrapping paper. "Last-minute wrapping?"

"Yup. Getting things ready for tomorrow." Amanda sounded distracted. As much as I didn't want to tell her I was bailing on Christmas Eve, I knew this was my opportunity.

"About tomorrow…" I hesitated, taking a sharp breath. Amanda sighed, and I was pretty sure she knew what I was going to say. "Adam invited me to have Christmas Eve dinner with his family. They do this fancy fish thing. I guess it's an Italian tradition or something. I told him I had plans, but I guess his mom really wants me to go...." I didn't have anything else prepared to say. I phrased it almost like I was looking for Amanda's permission. I wanted her to let me off the hook, tell me it was fine and that of course, I should have Christmas Eve dinner with my new boyfriend and his family. I waited, holding my breath, listening to the sound of wrapping on the other end of the phone.

The rustling paper sounds stopped, and there was more silence. Then Amanda sighed again and said, "Guess I don't need to finish wrapping your gift."

Just like that, the line went dead.

CHAPTER SEVENTEEN

I knew Amanda was mad, and to be honest, I didn't blame her. But I also didn't know what else to do. I told her as much in the dozen text messages that went unanswered over the rest of the afternoon. By dinnertime, I'd taken a turn towards resentment. Amanda was betraying me. I needed her support and her guidance. I wanted her to help me pick out my outfit for tomorrow and give me tips on how to do my hair. I wanted her advice on meeting Adam's family. Mostly, I wanted to feel like she was happy for me.

I was sulking in my room, surrounded by nearly every item of clothing I owned, when my mother walked in. She took one look around and sat down next to me on the bed. That was all it took for me to unravel. A half an hour later, I was still sobbing onto the front of her blouse.

"This is normal," my mother said, rubbing slow circles on my back with one hand. "It's hard when you get your first boyfriend. Amanda is used to being the most important person in your life. She's jealous, for probably lots of reasons."

I choked down a sob while my mother assured me this would pass. Amanda would realize she was being silly. Things would go back to normal. I was surprised at how comforted I was by my mother's words. I let her rub my back for a few more minutes, and then I asked her to help me pick out a formal outfit to wear to Christmas Eve dinner.

My mother leapt into action. She moved around the room, making piles of my clothes and then sorting those piles into new piles. She ultimately laid out a gray skirt I hadn't worn since picture day last year and an emerald-green sweater I'd bought while Christmas shopping with Amanda. I tried not to think about how Amanda rolled her eyes when I picked it up.

My mother laid the outfit out on my bed, and I couldn't help but agree that it looked both sophisticated and festive at the same time. My mother certainly had style.

Mom promised to help me with my hair and makeup before I left the next day, and it looked like she was glowing when she slipped out of my bedroom a little while later. It was as if our relationship had suddenly altered to a place where we could be friends. Maybe I was finally becoming the daughter that she'd always wanted me to be.

I checked my phone before climbing into bed, hoping to see an apology from Amanda. Instead, I found a short message from Adam telling me how excited he was for tomorrow. Despite how upset I was at Amanda, I couldn't help but smile. She'd been so wrong about Adam. He was clearly not the guy she'd assumed he was.

Maybe my mother was right. Maybe Amanda was actually just jealous of the fact that I had a boyfriend and she didn't. Maybe that was why she had been so anti-Adam all along. Or maybe she was jealous my winter formal night had been so much more amazing than the one she'd had. Maybe she was just mad that it was me instead of her.

When I woke up the next morning, I was instantly anxious. Despite the fact that Christmas was supposed to be a joyous holiday, it suddenly felt momentously daunting. I was already convinced there was no way Adam's family would like me. By the time I finished breakfast, I worked up a half-a-dozen scenarios that ended with Adam throwing me out of his house.

It didn't help that Amanda was still ignoring me. I sent her a text as soon as I woke up wishing her a happy Christmas Eve. I know how much she loves Christmas Eve, and I was hoping her excitement for the holiday would outweigh her annoyance at me from last night. Since it had been nearly three hours since I sent the text, however, it didn't appear that was going to be the case.

Adam told me to arrive at two in the afternoon. My mother started tackling my hair and makeup just after noon, and nearly two hours later, I was worried she would never be finished. I fidgeted in the uncomfortable dining room chair I was seated in.

"Relax," my mother said around the makeup brush she clenched in her teeth. "Men are used to women arriving late for important events." While I knew my mother was a fan of being fashionably late, I was less sure that was the best plan for the first time I was meeting Adam's entire family.

My mother could not be rushed, though. She moved steadily around me until a quarter of two, when she finally stepped back to admire her work. She was beaming at me, and I was almost sad to have to rush away from her. If I wasn't mistaken, I would swear there was pride in her eyes.

I ran into the bathroom to see her work for myself, and to be honest, I barely even recognized the girl staring back at me. My skin was smooth and even, and it seemed to radiate under the bathroom light. My mother had chosen soft pink tones that almost made it seem like I wasn't wearing makeup at all. She tamed my hair into an elegant updo that left just the most delicate curls hanging lose around my face. There wasn't a frizzy strand to be found.

When I slipped into the outfit she'd picked out, it was like I stepped out of a Lifetime Original Holiday Movie. My mother clapped her approval, and for the first time I could remember, she told me I looked beautiful.

The comment caught me off guard, and I almost forgot I was running late. I was still basking in the glow of her affection when she handed me the keys to her car.

"Home before midnight," she told me as she kissed my forehead. As she turned back into the kitchen, I thought I saw the glimmer of a tear in the corner of her eye.

It was 2:21, according to the clock on the dashboard of my mother's Nissan when I pulled up in front of Adam's house. There was a handful of cars parked in his driveway and a few more out on the street. I'd gotten six texts from Adam while I was driving to his house, starting at exactly two o'clock.

r u here??

where r you?

did you forget i said 2?

where r u????

sasha???

ur late.

Another text pinged on my phone as I got out of the car and straightened my skirt. I glanced down at the screen as I hurried up the walk. I expected it to be another text from Adam, but I was surprised to see it was from Amanda.

Merry Christmas Eve. Have fun at dinner, good luck.

I was still looking at the screen when the front door of Adam's house swung open.

"Finally!" Adam cried. The word sounded playful, but annoyance still seemed to flash in his eyes. He ushered me into the house and introduced me to almost two dozen people in a flurry of names and relationships I would never remember. His family was all gathered in a formal living room off the main hall. The room felt like a museum, the type of place where you look at things but can't touch them.

The oldest members of the family were on display on the various uncomfortable-looking couches, including a woman I was pretty sure Adam introduced as his great-great-aunt. The rest of the family stood around in small groups, talking in hushed voices.

Most of them were holding champagne flutes and barely acknowledged me as Adam introduced me to each one. The room felt stuffy, and there wasn't a hint of festive Christmas spirit. I quickly realized Adam and I were the two youngest people in the room by probably close to a decade. There were no children playing with toys or anxiously awaiting the arrival of Santa Clause. The atmosphere felt more like an important business dinner than a Christmas Eve party.

After the whirlwind introductions in the museum room, Adam led me into the kitchen where his mother was wearing an apron and managing several pots on the stove at once. Her blond hair was pulled back into a long French braid, but the pieces around her face had come loose and were starting to curl from the steam in a way I was all too familiar with.

She stopped and smiled, shaking my hand, which seemed too formal for her homey kitchen. The atmosphere was completely different than out in the living room. The kitchen was filled with the smells of holiday dinner, and Christmas carols were playing softly in the background. The kitchen was bright and bustling as Mrs. Lincoln moved from the stove to the oven and back again with graceful precision. I found myself hoping we could stay in the kitchen rather than venturing back into the cheerless living room.

To be polite, I offered Mrs. Lincoln a hand. She smiled, and I noticed she had the same deep dimples as Adam. She thanked me but insisted Adam and I go enjoy ourselves rather than be stuck in the kitchen.

Adam led me back into the living room. I caught a glimpse of the dining room, where a long table was elegantly set in what appeared to be holiday-themed china. A second table had been set up at the far end of the room so that the two tables formed a kind of T shape.

I let Adam lead me over to where his grandparents were seated. I stood awkwardly in front of them as Adam obediently answered questions about how his school year was progressing. They directed their questions to Adam, as if I were nothing more than a piece of furniture. After a while, I used a break in the conversation to lean close to Adam and ask him where the bathroom was. He pointed me down a long hallway, and I was relieved to escape from the stuffiness of the living room.

I ran some water over my hands. I hadn't realized I'd been clenching them so tightly, and they were slick with sweat. I pulled my phone out of my pocket and reread Amanda's text. I tapped out a reply and waited to see if she would answer immediately. When she didn't, I checked my reflection and fixed my lipstick the way my mother had showed me. Satisfied, I steeled myself and pulled the door open. I jumped back when I found Adam standing directly on the other side.

"Are you okay?" He worded it like he was concerned, but something else played across his face.

"Of course," I said, plastering what I hoped was a reassuring smile on my face. "I was just fixing my lipstick."

"If you didn't want to come, you didn't have to." Adam grabbed my hand and started leading me back toward his family.

"That's not it at all," I whispered to his back as we reentered the room. No one seemed to pay us any attention as we moved through the small crowd.

"You show up late and then you disappear off into the bathroom forever. That doesn't make it seem like you want to be here."

He said the words through gritted teeth. He looked hurt, and my heart melted. I felt terrible for being more concerned about myself than I was for his feelings.

"I'm sorry," I said, squeezing his hand. "I was just nervous and trying to look nice for you, that's all."

Adam didn't smile, but before he could say anything else, his mother came out and started herding people into the dining room. I followed Adam inside, and he pulled out a chair for me at the far end of the T-shaped table. He sat down next to me but immediately turned away to talk to his uncle. They weren't even speaking loud enough that I could pretend to be involved in the conversation.

Luckily, the food Mrs. Lincoln had prepared was delicious and I could busy myself with eating instead of talking. The first and second courses passed quickly. Between bites, I watched the quiet conversations taking place around me but didn't bother to try to involve myself with them. They all seemed mildly superficial, as if the family was mostly made up of strangers who were simply passing the time with meaningless small talk.

During the third course, I found myself wondering what Amanda's family would think of the way the Lincolns politely passed food around in near silence.

Christmas dinners at Amanda's were loud and rambunctious. There were always multiple conversations taking place, but the entire table was involved in all of them. In the same breath someone might loudly contribute to two or even three of the conversations, fighting to be heard over the person next to them doing the same.

No topic was off limits. Arguments about politics, debates over the best restaurants, even advice on upcoming business deals were all discussed with equal enthusiasm. Amanda's father would sit at the head of the table acting as some sort of moderator as the conversations whirled around him. Although it wasn't uncommon for the Attwoods to touch on hot-button topics during meals, it was always good-natured. No one ever left the table upset.

Picking at the shrimp during the fourth course, I realized how much I missed the rowdiness of the Attwoods' Christmas Eve dinners. I wondered if there was some sort of unspoken rule about what topics were safe to discuss in the Lincoln household.

It was pretty obvious that everyone seated around this table was walking on eggshells. I overheard at least three different people mention the cooler weather we'd been having lately. Another conversation dwelled on the weather in Florida, where someone apparently had just been vacationing. The conversations as a whole were mundane and pretty boring. I wasn't even upset that I was being left out.

While Adam passed the plate of haddock for the fifth course, he and his uncle discussed his college prospects. It was clear that at this point in his decision-making, Adam was only considering the strength of the school's baseball team. His uncle asked polite questions about what Adam wanted to major in and what he was thinking about doing after college.

I listened as Adam explained his hopes of playing minor league baseball. It sounded like Adam truly believed he was good enough to be recruited for a major league team, but he was trying to sound modest as he talked with his uncle. I hadn't seen Adam play yet, but based on the tight-lipped expression on his uncle's face as he listened to Adam's plan, he didn't seem to think Adam would be fulfilling this dream. His uncle made a less-than-subtle remark about Adam needing a back-up plan, but Adam didn't seem deterred.

During the sixth course, the woman seated across the table from us directed a similar line of questioning at me. It was the first time during the entire meal that anyone directly attempted to engage me in conversation.

I vaguely remembered Adam introducing this woman as Aunt Kate or possibly Aunt Sherry. She wore a bulky knit sweater in a dull brown that matched her lifeless-looking hair. Her equally dull brown eyes were framed by chunky black square glasses. She studied me over the tops of the frames as she asked about my future plans.

I told her I wanted to go to Columbia and that I planned to study engineering there. I was relieved to be questioned on a topic where

I didn't have to put much thought into the answer. I'd been planning to attend Columbia for as long as I could remember.

"Ambitious," the woman said, pushing her plate away from her to prepare for the final course. I couldn't tell if she was being sarcastic or not. Regardless, she turned away and didn't bother to ask me anything else.

By the time the final course was passed around, I was completely stuffed. When Adam handed me the platter of fried scallops, I couldn't fathom eating another bite. I passed the platter down the table, amazed that no one else was as full as I was. Had they all been starving themselves for days in preparation for this meal?

As I looked around the table, my eyes met Adam's. He looked disapprovingly down at my empty plate.

"You don't like my mother's cooking?" He kept his voice low and leaned toward me. I couldn't tell if it was hurt or anger building in his eyes.

"Your mother's cooking was delicious. I was stuffed after the fifth course. I just don't have any more room!" I tried to laugh, but the strain was too much for my stomach.

"Well, you shouldn't have eaten so much before you came over. It wouldn't have killed you to skip breakfast." Adam returned his attention to his plate. I stared at the side of his face. I couldn't decide if I was reading too much into his comment.

On the one hand, it could have been entirely innocent. No one would actually die from skipping one meal. Maybe he was just implying I should have planned ahead better. In fact, had I known there would be this much food, I would have skipped breakfast. I might have even skipped dinner the night before to prepare.

But on the other hand, the comment felt like more than that. I couldn't help but glance down at the way my stomach now bulged against the waistline of my skirt. I was obviously not in the best physical shape. At one hundred and thirty-five pounds, it was certainly clear I enjoyed my fair share of comfort foods. But I'd never considered myself overweight.

The comment buzzed in the back of my mind throughout the rest of the meal. I could hear Adam's words in my mind, and I puzzled over which way he meant them. When Mrs. Lincoln offered me a bowl of chocolate pudding, Adam didn't even allow me time to decline.

"She's fine, Mom," he said, taking the bowl Mrs. Lincoln had been offering me for himself. I hadn't planned on accepting the dessert, mostly because I couldn't have possibly fit even a single spoonful of pudding into my stomach, but I was still surprised by Adam's retort.

The dinner wrapped up around me. Thankfully, it appeared that dessert was the final event of the evening and we wouldn't be subjected to anymore painful pleasantries.

One by one, members of the Lincoln family left the table and made the rounds to say goodbye. Most of them skipped over me as they moved about the table, not even bothering to recognize my existence in the room. A few of them awkwardly shook my hand, and it was clear they couldn't remember my name in order to say goodbye to me properly, which was fine, since I didn't remember their names either. When most of the family had left the table and Mrs. Lincoln had denied my offer to assist her in cleaning up for the third time, I told Adam that I should probably be heading home.

He seemed unusually tense as I followed him to the door. He thanked me for coming over, and we stood awkwardly in the hallway behind the front door. I wondered if I had done something to upset him.

I couldn't recall having said or done anything he'd be offended by; in fact, I hadn't said much at all. If anything, I was the one who should be upset. He had basically called me fat during Christmas Eve dinner. After several uncomfortable seconds, Adam made up his mind and leaned forward to give me a goodbye kiss. I felt some of the tension release as I moved closer to him. When he stepped back and opened the door, it didn't feel like he was upset anymore. I thanked him for having me and wished him Merry Christmas.

As I settled myself into my car, I felt a rush of relief. Dinner hadn't gone at all like I'd expected. I was thankful to not feel like I needed to walk on eggshells anymore. I started to drive home, but something nagged at the back of my mind. In a last-minute decision, I jerked the car down the road that would take me to Amanda's house. I parked at the curb outside and hoped Amanda wouldn't close the door in my face when she saw me. I hesitated before ringing the bell. Christmas carols drifted out from inside the house, and started to relax.

"Since when do you ring the bell?" Amanda asked when she pulled the door open to reveal me standing sheepishly on the doorstep.

"I wasn't sure if I was welcome."

Amanda stepped back and opened the door wider to allow me past her.

"Everyone's welcome on Christmas Eve," she said with a smile, "even you."

Inside, the Attwood household was exactly as I knew it would be. Music played loudly, people were singing and smiling, everyone was in the Christmas spirit. Her family welcomed me with cheers and passed me a glass of eggnog. I collapsed on the floor next to Ben, who was giddy with Christmas Eve excitement.

"You missed dinner," Mrs. Attwood exclaimed. "Are you hungry? I can heat something up for you." She was already starting to stand up, prepared to head into the kitchen for me. I shook my head furiously and clutched my still-bulging stomach.

"I couldn't possibly eat. I had six of the seven fish courses at Adam's."

"Oh, how fancy!" Mrs. Attwood said, settling back into her seat.

Without missing a beat, she launched back into singing a verse of "Jingle Bell Rock." Amanda sat down beside me. I knew there was something she wanted to say, but as some kind of Christmas miracle, she decided to keep it to herself. Instead, she wrapped an arm around my shoulders, and we joined in on the sing-along.

I spent the rest of the evening engulfed in the type of Christmas cheer that was so obviously missing at Adam's house. By the time I got home, I had almost completely forgotten about the long hours I'd spent at Adam's house earlier in the day. My mother was waiting up for me when I walked through the door. I realized I'd forgotten to text her when I'd left Adam's and went to Amanda's. She buzzed around me, asking questions about Adam's house and family. I told her about the awkward way his family interacted and the delicious food Mrs. Lincoln served. Then I told her about the comments Adam had made at dinner. My mother fanned the air to shoo away my thoughts.

"I'm sure you're overthinking all that, Sasha. Adam's a nice boy; he wouldn't say something like that with the intention of hurting your feelings." With that, my mother changed the subject, apparently closing the book on my irrational overthinking.

At the time, I thought she was right. I was certain Adam was a nice boy. I figured I was just being too sensitive. Maybe I did just take the whole thing out of context.

Your mind can convince you of those types of things, you know. You can rewrite how something happened in your head and play it back however you want to.

I know that now.

Sometimes I wonder if that's what I did with the whole time. Maybe it was never the relationship I thought it was. Maybe I was constantly rewriting it. Maybe the whole thing was just something I made up.

After everything that happened, how can I be sure?

CHAPTER EIGHTEEN

On Christmas morning, I woke to the smell of cinnamon buns baking in the oven. I knew before I even opened my eyes that I would find my mother and Grandma June in the kitchen together. Christmas morning always made me feel like a little girl again, despite now knowing that Grandma June brought the presents and not Santa. I had long ago found the secret stash my mother hid in the spare bedroom of Grandma June's house. In a way, knowing Grandma June was part of the Christmas magic made it even more special.

I threw my robe over my shoulders and scurried out into the kitchen. Grandma June stood at the counter, kneading gingerbread dough. She was taller than my mother by a few inches, and her hair had long ago gone gray, but she was still every bit as beautiful as my mother. The sleeves of her maroon sweater were pushed up, and there was already a smudge of flour on her black pants. She smiled when she saw me and patted her hands clean on a dish towel.

"There's my favorite granddaughter! I thought you were never going to get out of bed. I was starting to worry we'd have to open presents without you!"

I folded myself around my grandmother's thin body. Even though she was taller than I was, I always felt like I might break her if I squeezed too hard.

Grandma June handed me a mug of hot chocolate with a candy cane sticking out of the glass. She'd been making me this peppermint hot chocolate drink on Christmas morning for as long as I could remember. I sipped the warm liquid and collapsed onto a stool opposite where my grandmother was working.

"So," she said, digging her hands back into the dough on the counter, "your mother tells me there's a new boy in your life these days."

I nodded shyly. I should have guessed my mother wouldn't be able to contain herself.

"His name is Adam, and we just started dating three days ago."

"Three days ago and I'm just hearing about it now?" Grandma June feigned shock. "You didn't even mention him when we were typing the other day."

Grandma June would not use the word texting. She stubbornly refused to use the form of communication for several years, but she had recently fallen in love with the convenience of being able to carry out a conversation regardless of what was going on around her. She now used her cell phone almost exclusively to text, though she thought the word "text" sounded ridiculous and called it "typing" instead.

"I guess I wanted to tell you in person, but someone ruined the surprise."

I pretended to glare at my mother, who was stirring a pot on the stove. She didn't look up, but she waved her hand dismissively.

"You got to tell me, I got to tell my mother. That's how having a mother works."

Although I wanted to be annoyed, I was secretly kind of excited that my mother had told Grandma June about Adam. I assumed that meant my mother was excited about it, and I couldn't remember the last time my mother had been excited to tell Grandma June anything about me.

"Well," Grandma June said, looking up from the dough, "tell me all about this young man."

"He's absolutely gorgeous," my mother said, without allowing me the chance to say a thing. "He's tall and dark and delicious. He's a big baseball star. Very popular. Our little Sasha is a lucky girl."

"Oh, Vanessa! Let the girl speak for herself!"

My mother continued as if my grandmother hadn't chastised her.

"He honestly looks like something out of a magazine. I couldn't believe it the first time he turned up at the house. I was hoping he was just a bit older than he is so I could scoop him up for myself!"

"Mother!" I cried, not bothering to hide that I was disgusted at the thought. My grandmother shook her head.

"She's always been like this, Sasha. I swear, I don't know where she got it from."

My mother pretended to mimic my grandmother behind her back. Grandma June winked at me like she knew exactly what her daughter was doing. She always said she had eyes in the back of her head.

I told my grandmother a little more about what Adam was like. She smiled as I described the way he'd asked me to the dance. A familiar giddiness crept into my voice as I described the winter formal to her.

"I'm sure you looked absolutely stunning," Grandma June said. "Did you take any pictures?"

"Oh! One of Adam's friends took one of us. She texted it to me the other day. Hang on!" I scrambled out of the kitchen and slid down the hall to my bedroom. I grabbed my phone off my bedside table and tapped the screen to wake it. As I rushed back down the hall, I had several "Merry Christmas" texts to respond to, including several from Adam.

I opened the photo of Adam and me at the dance. Adam's arm was wrapped securely around my waist, and my dress had a purple tint due to the DJ's flashing lights. The focus was slightly off, and the girl who'd taken the photo had cut off our feet. I would have framed the whole shot differently if I had taken it, but it was the only picture I had of Adam and me, and I was already in love with it.

Grandma June studied the photo carefully, a smile on her face.

"You looked absolutely lovely, sweetheart. And this Adam looks quite nice, as well."

I took my phone from Grandma June and settled back into my seat. Grandma June rolled out the dough for the gingerbread and carefully pressed cookie cutters into the sheet. She gently arranged them on a baking sheet before tucking them into the oven. As soon as she did, she began mixing ingredients for her famous sugar cookies.

Grandma June knew I hated to bake. There was a time where she assumed I would love it. After all, according to her, baking was a science. She spent many evenings attempting to teach me her secret recipes for various things, but I never really enjoyed the process. I much preferred to sit and watch her bake. I also enjoyed volunteering to test the finished products.

I sat and chatted with Grandma June while she finished her sugar cookie recipe and removed the gingerbread men from the oven, replacing them with the tray of sugar cookies. When the timer went off, Grandma June set them out to cool, and we all relocated to the living room.

When I was younger, Grandma June would wait until after we

exchanged presents to start baking. In recent years, we started waiting until later in the morning to do gifts. When we were finished the gift exchange, we'd make Christmas brunch before decorating the cookies she'd made. It was a simple tradition, not nearly as festive or as rowdy as those at the Attwood house, but certainly more intimate and enjoyable than the stuffiness of the Lincoln family tradition.

I unwrapped several new sweaters from my mother and a few books from my grandmother that I couldn't wait to read. My mother also got me the new tripod for my camera I had been begging for.

Last, I opened a tiny box wrapped in gold foil that was from both my mother and my grandmother. Inside, I found a delicate white-gold ring. Inlaid in the band were three sapphire stones. All three of us had been born in September, and sapphire is our birthstone. There was a stone to represent each of us.

I slipped the ring on my finger and held my hand out to admire it.

"Oh my god, this is so beautiful!" The delicate stones danced in the light as I moved my hand.

"Three beautiful, strong stones to represent three beautiful and strong women," Grandma June said, a smile lighting her face. I rushed across the room to hug her.

The ring was by far the most expensive and beautiful piece of jewelry I owned. I kept glancing at it throughout the rest of the day, and I couldn't help but smile each time it caught my eye.

My mother was right; I was a very lucky girl.

CHAPTER NINETEEN

The rest of Christmas vacation passed in a bit of a sugar-induced blur. Adam and his family left for a trip to Vermont, where they visited some other family and went skiing for the week. Adam texted me to tell me he wouldn't have cell service for most of the week. His family lived in the middle of nowhere, he told me. He said civilization barely made it that far north.

I spent most of the week with Amanda, and we quickly fell into our normal routine. We spent the post-Christmas days lounging around and watching Lifetime movies with unbelievable plots about their characters falling in love despite all odds. I was worried some of these plots might rekindle the debate about Adam, but Amanda continued to let the topic rest. The week passed quickly in the way that vacations always do.

One morning toward the end of the week, I woke up and realized I'd almost completely forgotten about Adam. I don't mean in a bad way; I just mean, my life had gone back to the way it had been before Adam and I were dating. My life was very simple again. Amanda and I alternated between her bedroom and mine, acting like the inseparable best friends we'd always been.

One night, while we were eating leftover Chinese food for the third meal in a row, Amanda put down the cardboard container of chicken lo mien she was eating.

"You're my best friend," she said, as if this was something I didn't know. She paused like she was waiting for me to answer a question she didn't ask.

"You're my best friend, too," I said.

"Good. I just want you to remember that." She picked the container back up and dug her fork back in, slurping some noodles into her mouth. I tried to puzzle through the meaning of what she had said. She returned her attention to whatever we were watching on TV at the time, and the conversation seemed to have ended as abruptly as it began.

On New Year's Day, I woke up midmorning after spending the night at Amanda's. We stayed up to watch the ball drop on TV while eating pizza and pints of Ben and Jerry's ice cream in our pajamas.

Still lying in bed, I reached for my phone and discovered almost a dozen messages from Adam. I glanced at the clock, which read 10:22. Adam had started texting me about forty-five minutes earlier.

hey beautiful, happy new year!

i hope u had a great night

i missed u

what did u do last night?

where r u?

r u ignoring me??

hello?????

what the hell sasha

did u go out with another guy last night???

is that why ur ignoring me??

what the fuck sasha!!

I read through the string of messages twice. Adam couldn't really think I was out with another guy, could he? I was still shocked by the fact that one guy wanted to spend time with me, never mind a second guy. The idea seemed ridiculous, but Adam seemed generally concerned and upset about the possibility. I quickly sent him a message apologizing. I explained I'd just woken up and that I was with Amanda. He responded almost immediately and asked where I was. I told him I was still at Amanda's house.

send a pic of u guys

I wasn't sure why he asked for a picture. It seemed like such a strange thing to request. I told him we'd just woken up and that we probably looked like shit. I couldn't imagine he really wanted to see us in our pajamas. Maybe he was under some delusion that girl sleepovers were sexy and that we really did have pillow fights in our underwear. I remembered a conversation we had with Andrew at lunch one day about that very thing. He refused to believe that we didn't sit around in lingerie and paint each other's toenails.

i don't care send a pic

I padded out to the kitchen and found Amanda at the counter making tea. I stood next to her and held my phone out in front of us. I snapped the picture before Amanda could protest. I knew she wouldn't be happy about having her photo taken before she applied any makeup.

"What the hell, Sash," she screeched, batting my phone away a second too late. "Why are you documenting my morning ugliness?"

"Adam asked for a picture of us." I was hoping I sounded nonchalant, like it didn't seem strange to me either. I forwarded the picture to Adam, trying not to focus on how unruly my hair looked. Amanda would hate the picture. Her mouth was open in surprise and the lack of makeup made her look pale. I plopped down at the kitchen table and took a banana out of the fruit bowl.

"He wanted a picture of us? Why?" Amanda abandoned her tea and was now standing over me with her hands on her hips. The disapproval radiated from her face.

"I don't know, he just asked for one. Maybe he misses me."

"Then why the hell did I have to be in it? He sure as hell doesn't miss me any!"

I shrugged and took a bite of my banana. Adam had looked at the photo but hadn't responded. I didn't have any better reason to offer to Amanda as to why he wanted the photo. Amanda crossed her arms in front of her chest and clicked her tongue.

"Seems pretty damn weird to me," she said, finally returning to her tea. I thought it was pretty weird too, but I wasn't going to admit that to Amanda. I didn't want to add any more fuel to her Adam-hating fire.

Amanda carried her tea over to the kitchen table and sat down across from me.

"You have to admit that's weird."

"I think you're reading too much into it. I'm sure he was just being playful."

Amanda raised her eyebrows over the rim of her mug. She took her time sipping her tea and contemplating her response. I bit my tongue, waiting for whatever she was going to say next. To my surprise, she just shook her head.

"Just be careful, Sash."

I laughed and told her she was being paranoid. What was there to be careful about? Back then, I truly did believe that. He was just a boy, after all. I couldn't imagine there was anything worth worrying about. I figured the worst thing he could do was break up with me.

Amanda was overreacting, a talent she excelled at. I was sure there was an innocent explanation for Adam requesting the photo. In fact, by the time I left Amanda's house later that afternoon, I stopped thinking about it all together. Girls sent boys photos all the time. It was all part of the flirty game of keeping them interested.

I texted with Adam off and on throughout the night while I caught up on some reading for English class. Everything about our conversation seemed so normal. He asked about my week and told me about skiing in Vermont. He promised to take me with him sometime so I could try skiing, despite my belief that I would not be coordinated enough to do very well. The conversation drifted through other topics, some serious, some playful. It wasn't long before I completely abandoned my book and focused my attention entirely on our messages.

I'll admit I was really enjoying the attention. It was nice to have someone want to know things about my life and ask questions about my opinions. Amanda was the only person I ever texted with this much, and she already knew everything there was to know about me. When we texted, we talked about gossip or movies or homework. We never had the type of deep conversations that two people just getting to know each other can have. I liked the way my conversations with Adam felt intimate, even though we weren't even in the same room.

At a quarter to one, I finally told Adam I needed to go to bed. He protested, saying he wasn't tired and wanted me to stay up with him, but I could feel how heavy my eyelids were becoming. I told Adam we'd see each other in just a few hours at school. After finally saying good night, I curled up into my pillow feeling unbelievably lucky.

Who would have imagined someone as wonderful as Adam would want to spend his time talking to someone like me? Even I couldn't believe it.

CHAPTER TWENTY

The next day, I was exhausted from staying up so much later than I normally would have, but I was happy to get back into the routine of school. I'm one of those people that really enjoys going to my classes. I like to be challenged and explore new things. I like the focused intensity of the classroom and the "Aha!" moment when suddenly a new concept just clicks into place in my mind. School is where I feel most comfortable. I hadn't given any thought to how being Adam's girlfriend might change my sacred routine.

Entering the school, I breathed a sigh of relief. I headed down the hall in the direction of my first class. When I reached the hallway that led to the gym, the sound of Adam's voice caught my attention.

Normally, I would have continued straight to my first class. On any other day, I would have arrived at my classroom early, sat down at my desk, and begun preparing my notebook for the lecture. I never would have glanced at the group of jocks hanging out in the entrance to the gym. I wouldn't have given them a second thought as I hustled by, eager to get my day started. But Adam's voice stopped me in my tracks, and I felt an internal pull to say hello to him.

I timidly took a step toward the group. It was mostly the same boys Adam had been with at the dance. I recognized a few of the girls from the dance also mixed into the crowd, and I took another step forward.

Uncertainty swept through me. I didn't belong here, and in the bright light of the school hallway, certainly Adam wouldn't want to be seen with me.

Changing my mind, I turned around, intending to hurry away before anyone noticed me lurking at the end of the hall. I didn't want to become that creepy girl who was stalking Adam or something.

But before I could disappear back into the throng of students headed deeper into the school, Adam called my name. The group parted and allowed me entry to the inner part of the circle. Adam draped an arm casually over my shoulder and planted a kiss on my cheek. He resumed his conversation without missing a beat. I perched awkwardly beside him, unsure about what I was supposed to be doing. Held in place by his arm and surrounded by his teammates, I had no choice but to observe the conversation happening around me.

I began to fidget uncomfortably. I needed to get to class so I could get ready to take notes. I had only wanted to say hello to Adam. I turned to Adam and whispered to him that I needed to get going to class.

"The bell hasn't even rung yet."

"I know, but I like to get there early."

Adam's arm suddenly felt heavier around my shoulders.

"Why? Who's in your class that you need to get there early for?"

I tried to explain that it wasn't anyone was in my class; it was that I had to get my things ready. He stared at me, as if completely unaware there was anything that ever needed to be done prior to the bell ringing.

"You go to class early so that you can get ready for class?"

I nodded. My cheeks started to flame a little as I realized how nerdy it sounded when it was worded that way. Adam stared at me, his eyes moving back and forth between mine for several seconds. After what felt like an eternity, he dropped his arm from my shoulders and kissed me gently on the cheek.

"Have a good class."

"I'll see you in chem," I told him. I could feel his eyes on me as I hurried down the hallway. I knew I would be cutting it close now to get my notes set up properly before the bell rang.

Normally, I would have used several colored pens to create different note sections on the page and label each one. Knowing I wouldn't have time to be as creative as normal, I rushed to simply set up the page without getting too fancy. As I worked, I couldn't shake the feeling that I was being watched. I glanced around the room, but no one was paying any more attention to me than they had a week and a half ago.

When the bell rang, I watched the rush of students push through the doorway to avoid being marked tardy. I had the sense of being watched again, and I could have sworn I'd seen Adam standing outside in the hallway. But when the doorway finally cleared, the hallway was empty. I told myself I was just seeing Adam everywhere now because I wanted to. There was no reason for him to be in the advanced placement English wing. I turned my attention toward my English teacher, happily focusing my mind on class.

Heading to third period, I was surprised to find I was a little nervous. Would things be different between Adam and me now that we were dating? I settled into our table and arranged my notebooks as I always did. When Adam entered the classroom, my eyes were drawn to him just as they had been on the first day of class. The only difference was that this time, Adam's eyes were locked on mine, too.

He slid onto the stool next to mine and planted a kiss on my cheek. I glanced around to see if anyone had noticed the display of affection. It's not that it was unwelcome; it just seemed so out of place in class. Adam leaned over and pulled my notebook across the table toward him.

"Is this what you get to class early to do?" He fanned the previous pages, revealing that nearly every page was designed in a similar way.

"Yes. It helps me stay organized and find what I need to later when I'm studying." The embarrassment crept in as I defended my nerdy qualities. Adam eyed my notebook skeptically.

"It looks more confusing to me," he said.

I shrugged and pulled the notebook back toward me. The stones on my new ring caught the bright lights of the chem lab. Adam reached for my hand.

"What's this?" he asked, angling my hand toward him.

"My mom and grandma gave it to me for Christmas! Sapphire is all our birthstones. Isn't it pretty?" I fluttered my fingers, making the stones glitter. Adam wrinkled his nose.

"Why aren't you wearing the ring I gave you?"

"I am, see!" I pulled the chain of my necklace out of my shirt, revealing his class ring.

"Why aren't you wearing it on your finger?" He crossed his arms.

"I can't wear it on my finger, Adam; it's way too big." I slipped my finger through the ring dangling from the chain.

"Whatever," Adam said. I could hear the moodiness in his voice.

Before I could say anything else, Mr. Carter came into the room and welcomed everyone back from winter break. Adam doodled in his own notebook as Mr. Carter outlined the plans for the remainder of the term.

I couldn't help but watch Adam's movements throughout the class. I found them even more distracting now than I had in the past. It was as if everything he did sent sparks through the table to me.

I forced my concentration to remain on Mr. Carter's lecture and my own notes, even when I could feel Adam's eyes on me. He seemed to be watching me far more than normal, or at the very least, I was more aware of it now.

When the bell rang, Adam didn't immediately bolt toward the door like he normally did. He lingered near the edge of our lab table waiting for me to pack up my things.

His annoyance about the ring seemed to have tapered off during class. We left the classroom together, following the crowd toward the lunchroom.

"Do you ever get tired of being so smart?" Adam asked, reaching for my hand.

"What do you mean?"

"All those notes and paying so much attention in all your classes. Doesn't that get boring?"

I went to laugh, but I realized he wasn't kidding.

"I just really like school."

"Do you really want to go to Columbia?" Adam and I walked through the doors of the cafeteria. I assumed he would release my hand so we could go to our respective tables on opposite sides of the lunchroom, but he didn't.

"Yes, I've always wanted to go to Columbia."

Amanda and Andrew were already arguing at my table.

"Columbia's baseball team isn't very good."

I couldn't hold back my laughter this time.

"Yeah, but I'm not picking my college based on their baseball statistics."

Adam led me across the cafeteria to the long table where he sat with his baseball teammates. He slid onto the bench and looked up at me funny when I didn't immediately sit down.

"Oh," I said as the lightbulb clicked on inside my head, "you want me to sit over here with you?" I hadn't even considered this as a possibility. Adam nodded and patted the space beside him.

"Where else would you sit?"

"Well, I was going to sit at my table over there like I always do."

I looked across the lunchroom, expecting Amanda and Andrew to be almost screaming at each other by now. Instead, I found Amanda watching me.

"Don't be ridiculous," Adam said, grabbing my arm and tugging me toward the table. "You have to sit here with me." I allowed myself to be pulled onto the seat, and I set my things down on the table. Looking around, I noted nearly all the players were flanked by their respective girlfriends.

I sat for a minute and then pushed myself to my feet. Adam looked up at me, concerned, but I assured him I was only going to buy my lunch.

On my way out of the lunch line, I stopped next to Amanda. Although I could tell she knew I was standing there, she did not acknowledge me.

"I'm going to sit with Adam today," I said softly. Maura clapped her hands together and let out a little squeal.

"I heard all about you two at the dance!" She winked in my direction and gave me a thumbs-up.

"Amanda? Did you hear me?"

Amanda turned toward me, and we locked eyes. I knew she had something to say, but just as she opened her mouth, I felt an arm slide around my waist.

"Everything okay, Sash?" Adam asked. He hugged my hips against him, making me feel unstable. Amanda's eyes slid judgmentally up and down Adam. She scoffed and turned her back to me, pretending to be engrossed in the conversation happening next to her. After a second, I let Adam lead me back to his table.

"What's her problem?" Adam asked, as we settled back onto the bench next to his teammates.

"I'm not sure."

"It doesn't seem like she likes me."

"I'm sure that's not it," I said, but even I knew it didn't sound convincing.

After lunch, Adam insisted on walking me to my last class. He promised to meet me after school to drive me home. I tried to tell him he didn't have to, but he wouldn't listen to my protest. Sure enough, after class I found Adam waiting outside my classroom as if he'd never walked away.

When Adam pulled his truck up outside my house, he leaned over to kiss me. I allowed myself to be engulfed by him. It was so easy to forget about everything else when Adam was kissing me. Amanda's judgment suddenly didn't matter. The only thing that mattered was kissing Adam more.

When I finally slipped through the door, my mother was waiting for me in the kitchen.

"Got a ride home from school today, did you?" She was almost giddy with excitement. I blushed, guessing she'd been watching us out the window again. "He's such a lovely boy. You really got lucky with that one, young lady."

CHAPTER TWENTY-ONE

The Saturday after we went back to school, I told Adam I was going out to take pictures. He insisted on joining me.

I loaded my new tripod and my camera bag into his truck, and he drove me to my favorite spot for landscape shots, which was about half an hour outside of town. I liked the spot because it was tucked away from everything, just far enough off the beaten path that there weren't usually a ton of other people poking around. I didn't have to worry about someone accidentally walking into a shot I was preparing.

Adam parked his truck along the field and helped me carry my equipment down to the wood line. Another reason I love this area is because it has a little bit of everything. The field along the road is wide with tall grass that sways gently in the wind. In the summertime, the field is filled with colorful wildflowers. The wood line provides sharp angles and long shadows that I can play with to create dramatic images. Just beyond the tree line, there's a small brook that runs down along a rocky creek bed. Depending on the time of day, the light trickles through the tree branches and dances over the water.

Some of my favorite pictures have been taken right there. One of them even received honorable mention in a youth photography contest hosted by National Geographic.

I've never told anyone about that before now. I used to submit my photos to lots of different contests. I was too embarrassed to tell anyone I was doing it, but I always got a little thrill out of shipping off my entry. I haven't submitted anything in a long time though. I guess that's just one more thing that I lost interest in doing.

Usually when I got to this spot, I'd wander around with my equipment until inspiration struck me. Then I would carefully set up my tripod and equipment and try to capture the vision I was seeing in my mind. But as I trekked my camera bag through the trees, I felt a slight pressure having Adam with me. He said he wanted to see me in my element, but it felt more like I was being judged.

After we walked for about half a mile along the brook, Adam asked me why I hadn't taken any pictures yet. I tried to ignore the distinct sound of disappointment in his voice as I told him I was searching for the right spot.

"Every spot looks the same," Adam said as he ripped a leaf off a low-hanging branch and started tearing it to pieces. I flinched, feeling defensive of my special place. To me, the area changed minute to minute. The lighting could shift, the wind could blow. Nothing stayed the same, and it was all incredibly beautiful.

Feeling rushed, I picked a spot where some shadows were stretching out across a rockier part of the brook. I took my tripod from Adam and carefully set it up on the far bank. Once it was set up, I positioned my lens. I was making adjustments when Adam came up behind me.

"Can I see the picture?"

"I haven't even taken it yet."

"What do you mean you haven't taken it yet?"

The obvious shock in Adam's tone made me glance over my

shoulder. Adam was gaping at me, his mouth actually hanging open.

"Sometimes the shots take a while to set up." I turned back to my camera, trying to ignore Adam, who had begun kicking small rocks in the direction of my tripod. I adjusted a few more settings, trying to find the exact image I wanted to capture.

"Nothing's even moving!" Adam exclaimed, no longer even attempting to hide the annoyance in his voice. "It's not like you've got to wait for that rock to crack a smile."

I felt my motivation dwindling. I snapped a couple of pictures, though I knew they weren't at all what I was looking for, and started to disassemble my tripod.

"Maybe we should go."

"All this for just one picture? Jesus Christ, how annoying." Adam picked up my tripod and started walking back in the direction of the truck. I was surprised by the careless way he walked through the woods, not seeing or hearing all the beauty around him. He stalked out into the field and didn't even notice the deer he startled in doing so. She took off running for the trees so fast I didn't have time to get my camera up to try to get a picture of her. I always made sure I moved carefully through the woods, in case I got the opportunity to photograph any of the animals that lived there.

By the time I made it to the car, Adam had already climbed inside. I hurried to slide in beside him, sensing he was growing impatient.

"I'm hungry," Adam announced a few minutes later as he steered the truck into the parking lot of a local restaurant.

My phone vibrated in my pocket. I was in a group chat with Amanda and Maura and some of the other people from our lunch table. Maura sent a message to the group reporting a ridiculous incident at play rehearsal when Andrew apparently said vagina when he meant to say Virginia.

I followed Adam inside the little mom-and-pop shop, and we

were escorted to one of the eight tables in the dining room. It was about an hour after the lunch rush and too soon for a dinner crowd, so we had the place to ourselves. A girl I recognized from school but didn't know personally brought us menus, despite the fact that we'd both probably eaten here enough times to be able to recite the menu backwards in our sleep.

Adam studied it anyway, as if he wasn't sure what he was going to get. I wasn't very hungry but decided I'd get a basket of fries. When I ordered it, Adam eyed me with a look of disgust.

"A small basket of fries," he told the waitress, holding his thumb and pointer finger together to emphasize the size.

My cheeks flared as Adam disapproved of my unhealthy eating habits. My phone vibrated against the table where I'd set it down. I checked the display, noting several more messages had been added to the group chat about Andrew's Freudian slip.

Adam was watching me. I returned the phone to the table without opening any of the incoming messages, but it vibrated again almost immediately.

"Well, aren't you just Little Miss Popular," Adam said. He was smiling, but his tone didn't match his expression. He reached across the table and snatched my phone from where it lay. "Who is it that's more interesting than spending time with me?"

Adam skimmed the home screen of my phone and I watched as his eyes clouded over with anger.

"Who is Andrew, and why is he sending you so many messages?"

"Andrew is just a guy I know from the drama club, and he's not really sending messages to me; it's a group chat."

Adam began swiping through my phone, which I never bothered to lock. My mother never cared who I was texting, and I didn't have any prying younger siblings to guard against. I watched as Adam scanned through the list of people I text with. He opened several chats, checking the contents before returning to the main list. He started swiping through my call log and the other apps on my phone.

"What are you looking for?" I asked him, reaching for my phone. There was nothing on it I was ashamed of, but the aggressive way Adam was swiping through it made me uncomfortable. He leaned back so the phone was out of my reach.

"What's on here that you're trying to hide?" Adam glared at me over the top of my phone, relentless in his search.

"There's nothing on there. I don't even know what you're trying to find." Defeated, I sat back in my chair with my arms crossed. Adam scrolled through my contacts again, questioning every male name he came across.

When he finally finished, he tossed the phone across the table so it landed in front of me with a thud. I was aware that since there was no one else in the small restaurant, our waitress had probably seen the entire encounter. I flushed at the idea of her thinking I was attempting to sneak around behind Adam's back. Even the thought of it seemed completely crazy.

Adam leaned back in his chair, clearly still annoyed. I wasn't sure why he seemed angry to have found that I wasn't doing anything wrong. When the waitress came with our food, she set our plates down without meeting my eye. She seemed to hurry away from the table, not even checking to make sure we had everything we needed.

I reached for the French fries in front of me, and Adam scoffed.

"You're not really going to eat those, are you?" I looked from Adam to the fries, confused.

"Of course I am. I ordered them." My hand was still hovering over the small mound of golden fries. Adam rolled his eyes.

"If I were you, I'd only eat a few," he said, before turning his attention to his own burger. My hand fell to the table as I processed the implication. At Christmas Eve dinner, I'd convinced myself I was being too sensitive about Adam's comments, but this time I was certain Adam was saying I was overweight. Tears were stinging the corners of my eyes, but I willed them away.

I focused my attention instead on ignoring the delicious smell of fried food wafting from the dish sitting in front of me. I watched Adam finish his burger before he began to pick at my fries. I never ate a single one.

When Adam was finished, the waitress removed our plates. Adam made a comment to her about how he knew I shouldn't have ordered French fries because I was just going to waste them. I fought back tears as I watched the girl walk away with my uneaten food.

I followed Adam out to his truck and slid silently into my seat. Adam drove me home, suddenly seeming to be in a much better mood. When we arrived at my house, he kissed me goodbye as if everything were normal. I smiled when he said he would see me tomorrow and told him I'd text him in a while.

When I got inside the house, I wondered again if I was being oversensitive. Maybe Adam was just looking out for my health. After all, everyone knew those fries were drenched in oil and probably other unhealthy chemicals, too.

I thought about asking Amanda what she thought, but I didn't want to give her another reason to hate Adam, especially if I was overreacting. She was very sensitive toward weight remarks, and I imagined even if I was being oversensitive, Amanda was not the right person to ask.

My phone beeped in my hand, and I expected to find another onslaught of group messages. Instead, I read a message from Adam, telling me how much fun he had watching me take pictures. I laughed at the screen. I was positive "fun" was the last word Adam could use to describe the afternoon in the woods. It was certainly the last word I would use. I would not plan to take him with me the next time I went out to my special place.

I clicked over to catch up with the messages from the group, but

I was surprised to see it wasn't there anymore. I scrolled through my inbox, looking for the block that would belong to the group text, but it was gone. I opened my contacts to send Amanda a message, asking if I somehow got deleted from the group because I was taking too long to respond. Just as I was about to click on her name, I noticed that Andrew's contact, which had been below Amanda's in my phone for two years now, was gone.

I stared at the spot where the contact should have been, which now skipped right from Amanda Attwood to Cheryl Monroe. There was no Andrew. In his frantic search of my phone, Adam must have accidentally deleted Andrew's number.

That's what I told myself, anyway. I told myself it was an accident. I never even bothered to ask Adam about it. I just assumed he hit a wrong button. It wasn't until later, when I realized I was missing the number for my Spanish tutor, Matt, that I discovered every male contact in my phone book had been deleted.

Even after I noticed Adam attempted to delete all the other males from my life, I never thought to say anything to him. I guess I hadn't seen the point. It would just upset him, and he was right. Why did I really need all those guys' phone numbers? It just seemed easier to move on.

CHAPTER TWENTY-TWO

I didn't know what to expect from my first Valentine's day as someone's girlfriend. I was nervous for weeks leading up to the date.

What kind of gift was Adam going to be expecting? I didn't want to give him anything too romantic, because that seemed clingy, but I didn't want to give him anything too generic, because that didn't seem like I'd put any effort into his gift.

I'd been obsessing over the topic, asking anyone who would listen for advice. My mother told me Valentine's Day was strictly a holiday for men to dote on women. She told me not to bother getting Adam a gift at all.

"There's a reason all the Valentine's gifts are pink and girly," she said, pointing to a large bouquet of pink roses that had arrived the day before from one of her latest boyfriends.

Grandma June's advice had been to ignore my mother.

"Don't listen to your mother when it comes to matters of the heart, sweetie," she said. "That woman wouldn't know love if it bit her on the ass."

When I asked her what she thought I should get Adam, she told me to listen to my heart. I found this advice equally unhelpful.

Oddly enough, it was actually Amanda who gave me the best idea, though I don't think it was her intention.

"He only actually cares about baseball," she said, and the dig was not lost on me. "Just get him a shirt or something."

Although it was designed to be an insult, Amanda was actually pretty spot-on. I remembered a baseball hat Adam had nearly bought himself while we were Christmas shopping. It wasn't a romantic gift, but I thought it would be something he'd like.

On Valentine's Day morning, Adam arrived at my house earlier than normal to pick me up for school. He came to the door carrying a large bouquet of carnations and a large teddy bear.

He smiled goofily as he handed the treasures to me. I carried the flowers into the kitchen and arranged them in a vase next to the ones for my mother. I sat the teddy bear between the two arrangements and snapped a picture of them with my phone. I posted the picture to my Facebook page, and before I even closed the app, the photo had already been liked multiple times.

I carried the little red gift bag into the living room where Adam was waiting. I tried to ignore my nerves as I handed it to him. He pulled out the ball cap and broke into a grin.

"This is the hat I wanted for Christmas! Thanks, Sash!" He put the hat on and adjusted the brim. He was smiling widely, and I felt myself relax.

Adam took my hand and led me out to the truck. He chattered happily as we drove to school, and I congratulated myself on successfully passing an important girlfriend test.

Walking through the school was like walking through a Hallmark store. Balloons, flowers and teddy bears were everywhere you looked.

Amanda was in an especially foul mood when I sat down next to her in our first-period class.

"Where's your bouquet?" She was wearing a black sweater that harshly contrasted all the red and pink surrounding her.

She'd never been a big fan of Valentine's Day. She claimed it was because it was overly commercialized, but I think deep down it was because she'd never had a valentine.

"Adam gave me my gift this morning," I said, dropping into my seat. "I didn't need to bring it to school."

"I figured you would have wanted to show off," she said bitterly. I tried to ignore the comment.

When Mrs. Harris passed around homemade heart-shaped cookies, I thought Amanda was going to gag.

I couldn't pretend I wasn't happy to get away from her for the rest of the day. I'd never understood Amanda's hatred toward the romantic holiday. It was nice to see so many people in love and happy. Even prior to this year, I'd always liked that it celebrated happiness.

When I arrived in chem class later that afternoon, I'd managed to forget all about Amanda's sour attitude.

Mr. Carter had placed a worksheet and two pairs of gloves at each of our workstations. When the class had settled in, he reiterated that today's lab required the use of protective equipment.

"We don't have a ton of extra gloves," Mr. Carter yelled over the noise that erupted as we started our lab. "Try not to rip the pairs you've been given!"

To avoid getting my sapphire ring snagged in the thin latex, I slipped it off my finger and placed it in the center of my notebook. I snapped on my gloves and quickly set to work.

Adam was especially enthusiastic during lab. He happily participated in the collection of materials and seemed incredibly interested in the outcome of the different chemical combinations. He even volunteered to document our results.

When we had finished our lab and cleaned up our tables, I stripped my gloves off into the trashcan. Returning to our station, I went to retrieve my ring from where I'd left it. It wasn't there. Panicked, I searched the table and the floor around our station. I was digging through my backpack when Adam returned from the bathroom.

"Have you seen my ring?" I asked him, the panic overwhelming my voice.

"What ring?"

"The sapphire one! The one I always wear."

Adam gazed across the table and then sat down.

"Oh, that ring. I don't remember seeing it," he said. "Are you sure you had it on?"

"Of course I had it on! I always have it on!" I turned my purse upside down on the workstation.

"Well, I don't remember seeing it. Maybe you lost it." Adam was packing his bag in anticipation of the bell ringing.

"I couldn't have lost it. It was right here." I flipped the pages of my notebook, though I knew there was no way the ring could have ended up on a different page.

"Well, it's not here now, so it sounds like you lost it." The bell rang, and Adam stood. He watched me, waiting for me to join him for the walk to lunch.

"It has to be here. I'm going to keep looking for it."

Adam shrugged and headed out into the hallway.

Mr. Carter helped me search every inch of the classroom, but I never found my ring. I was too devastated to even go to lunch. I couldn't believe the ring was gone. I was positive I'd placed it safely on my notebook and completely out of the way, despite Adam denying having seen it there.

"Maybe someone in the class stole it," I said to Adam on the phone later that night.

"Why would anyone steal that thing?" Adam said. He sounded bored, and I felt a pang of selfishness. I'd torn my bedroom apart, just in case Adam was right and I had forgotten to put my ring on this morning. When I didn't say anything, Adam added, "Guess now you can wear my ring instead."

I never found my sapphire ring, Doc. I searched every inch of the school; I turned my backpack and purse inside out. I checked the lost-and-found and even put up a few flyers around the science wing. I know I was wearing it at school that day, but I still scoured the house, just in case.

I never found it.

At some point, I gave up hope of finding it. Looking back now, I have to assume someone took it. There's no other explanation. Was it Adam? I guess I'll never know. I want to believe that it wasn't, but now I'm not so sure.

CHAPTER TWENTY-THREE

For years, my grandmother and I had been having dinner together on the last Sunday of every month. It was our standing tradition. Grandma June called it "girl time," even though, technically, every time I saw my grandmother was girl time. This was an opportunity for just the two of us to get together and catch up without anyone else around. We always let the tradition lapse a little during the holidays, but usually we would get back on track quickly and schedule our first dinner of the year for February.

Grandma June sent me a message on Thursday afternoon to remind me of our dinner plans. I was seated next to Adam on the tailgate of his truck when the text came through. I knew Adam was reading over my shoulder, and I didn't bother to try to shield the screen from him.

"Who are you having dinner with?" Adam said, leaning closer to my phone to see the screen in the bright sunlight. I stuffed the phone back into my pocket without responding.

"Just my grandmother. We have dinner together on the last Sunday of every month."

Adam knit his eyebrows together. "No, you don't," he said. "You usually have dinner at my house on Sundays."

"Well, we don't usually do it over the holidays because things are already hectic enough, but the rest of the year we try to have dinner at least once a month."

"Well, are you going to tell her you already have plans for this Sunday?" Adam asked. I turned toward him, using my hand to shield my eyes from the sun.

"What are you talking about? The only plan I have for this Sunday is dinner with Grandma June."

Adam crossed his arms firmly across his chest.

"No, you have dinner at my house on Sundays. You've done so every Sunday since we started dating. My parents are expecting you."

"It hasn't been every Sunday, Adam. And this is my grandmother. I'll have dinner at your house next week." I tried to lean into him, but he pulled away from me, sliding off the tailgate. He stood in front of me with his hands clenched at his sides.

"I can't believe you would blow me off like that. How do I even know that's actually your grandmother's number? Maybe it's some other guy who you entered into your phone with a false name so I wouldn't know who you were texting with." Although he was keeping his voice steady, Adam's eyes were filled with rage. The muscles in his jaw tensed while he spoke.

"That's insane! Of course it's my grandma I'm talking to! Why on Earth would you say such a thing?" Adam had made some crazy assumptions before, but this was by far the most ridiculous one.

"If it's really your grandmother, then she'll understand why you can't have dinner with her this Sunday night."

I stared at Adam in disbelief.

"You want me to ditch my own grandmother?"

"No, I want you to keep your promise to me," Adam said. He held my stare, daring me to continue to argue with him. "Your *grandmother* will understand." Adam used his fingers to put air quotes around the word "grandmother," proving he was still under the impression I was covering up some secret boyfriend.

I watched that muscle work in his jaw. I knew there was no way I could win this argument. I knew there was nothing I could do to convince Adam it was actually Grandma June I was meeting for dinner. Once he had an idea in his head, I knew I was better off to just give in.

"Fine," I said softly, pulling the phone out of my pocket again. Adam watched the screen as I slowly typed out an apology. I told my grandmother I accidentally made other plans for this Sunday night and asked her for a rain check. As I hit send, I hoped she actually would understand.

She responded a few minutes later and assured me we'd catch up soon. She seemed happy enough to reschedule. Hopefully, she wasn't too upset I had wanted to cancel.

"See," Adam said, settling himself back down on the tailgate next to me. "I told you she would understand." He reverted back to the casual, fun-loving Adam as quickly as he had become the angry-and-upset Adam. Sometimes the sudden transition made my head spin.

I nodded, knowing there was no point in talking about the matter any further.

On Sunday, I stood on Adam's doorstep just before five. Adam's father opened the door, looking surprised to see me.

"Oh, hello, Sasha," he said. "I didn't realize you were coming over tonight." I hesitated. Adam had said his parents were expecting me. Was I wrong, or had I detected a hint of annoyance in Adam's father's voice?

"Uh, sorry, Mr. Lincoln, Adam told me to come over for dinner." I shifted my weight from foot to foot uncertainly. It sure felt like Mr. Lincoln didn't want to let me into the house. After a minute that felt like an hour, Mr. Lincoln allowed the door to swing open wide enough for me to pass by him.

As I started down the hallway toward the kitchen, I thought I heard him sigh behind me. Adam wasn't in the kitchen, but Mrs. Lincoln was standing at the stove, shaking salt into a large pot of water.

"Oh, Sasha, hi! Adam didn't tell us you were coming over tonight. He's in the backyard; why don't you head out there and let him know dinner will be ready in ten minutes? Are you hungry?"

"Yes, ma'am," I said as I crossed the kitchen to the sliding door that led to the backyard. Anger was bubbling inside me, and my cheeks were hot. Adam lied to me. I marched out into the evening sunshine and spotted him throwing a baseball against a net. The net caused the ball to shoot back at him at odd angles. I'd watched him practice this way before.

"Adam! What the hell!" I wasn't quite yelling, but it was probably the loudest he'd ever heard me. He paused throwing the ball and turned toward me.

"What? What's up?" Adam watched me stalk toward him.

"Your parents had no idea I was coming over tonight! You told me they were expecting me! You made me cancel on Grandma June to be here!"

"Oh, whatever," Adam said casually, shrugging and turning back toward the net. "Guess they forgot." He threw the ball against the net and caught it in his glove.

I stood there fuming. Adam didn't even care he'd ruined my plans with Grandma June. I was so mad I couldn't even think straight. I just stood there in the yard watching Adam play catch with himself. I was debating just leaving when his mother called us inside for dinner.

Conversation didn't seem to flow around the table the same way it usually did. I mostly sat in silence, staring at my pasta while Adam and his father discussed the upcoming baseball season. After dinner, I helped Mrs. Lincoln clear the table. I tried to apologize to her for dropping in unexpectedly. Mrs. Lincoln waved off my apology and told me I was always welcome. Even though she said it, I didn't know if I totally believed her.

Adam was annoyed when I told him I had to leave shortly after dinner.

"You're just going to eat and then leave?" He had suggested we watch a movie, but I really wasn't in the mood.

"My mother made me promise I'd be home early tonight," I said. The lie came easier than I thought it would. In reality, my mother never cared how late I was at Adam's house. She probably wouldn't even be mad if I stayed all night. But I was still angry at Adam for making me miss dinner with Grandma June. I wanted some space and some time to fume.

"Fine," Adam said, walking me to the door. I was surprised that he didn't put up more of an argument, but I was relieved I only had to tell him one lie. I was focused on leaving, and I walked right by Adam on the doorstep.

Suddenly, my head wrenched backwards with force that caused my neck to crack. Adam grabbed the end of my braid and used it to pull me backwards. Instinctively, I yelped and made a grab for his hands. I tried to pry his finger loose from my hair, but he didn't let go. He held my braid firmly, and all I could do was allow him to drag me backwards toward the doorstep.

"Don't walk by me without giving me a kiss," he said through clenched teeth.

"Adam! Stop, you're hurting me!" My fingers clawed desperately at his fists. Finally, the tension on my hair lifted, and I was able to fully stand. I massaged my scalp through my hair and stared at Adam standing on the step. "What the hell, Adam!" Even though I was upset, I kept my voice low so Adam's parents wouldn't hear me.

"You don't get to just leave without kissing me goodbye," he said.

"That hurt a lot." I continued to rub the back of my head.

"Oh, don't be a baby, Sasha. I was just joking around with you. I was just mad you were going to leave without kissing me goodbye."

"I'm sorry, I wasn't thinking." I took a tentative step toward him and pecked his lips with my own. Before I could pull away, Adam wrapped one arm around my back and the other around my shoulders, pressing his hand against the sore spot on the back of my head. He held me against him and forced our mouths together. I dutifully allowed his tongue to probe my mouth.

When he released me, I stumbled backwards and nearly fell.

"Now that was a proper kiss goodbye," he said with a smile.

CHAPTER TWENTY-FOUR

My mom truly believed I was the luckiest girl alive. I couldn't help but wonder if that was because my mother couldn't believe someone like Adam Lincoln would be interested in someone like me.

Adam was exactly the type of guy my mother would have dated. He was handsome and popular and talented. My mother would have eaten that up when she was my age. Maybe that's why she constantly reminded me how lucky I was to have Adam.

"Don't let that boy get away," she'd say each time he came to pick me up or drop me off. It's not like I needed reminding. I was still equally shocked that Adam had selected me out of all the potential girls at Baymont High School. Every time I passed one of the gorgeous, popular girls in the hallway, I found myself wondering what Adam saw in me when he could have one of them.

Are you thinking the same thing? When I walked in here this afternoon, did you look me up and down and think, "What the hell was that boy thinking?" I know this is supposed to be a judgment free place, you've made that perfectly clear, but you're human. I can't imagine it didn't cross your mind.

I know what I look like sitting here. I haven't washed my hair in a few days, but this French braid is no match for my rebellious frizz. Being cooped up here has made my skin even paler and duller than usual, and this oversized gray sweatshirt does nothing for anyone's figure. Not that I have much of a figure anymore. I've lost so much weight, my mother says a slight breeze might knock me over. If I had anything that resembled feminine curves before, they're long gone.

I look the part of a crazy person now, for sure. It must be hard for someone like you to picture me any other way. Even though I was rarely successful, I used to try, at least. I tried to be the perfect girl I knew Adam wanted. I wore the clothes he liked and tried to do my hair the way he thought looked best.

I don't blame Adam for being disappointed in how I looked any more than I blame my mother. The two of them wanted what was best for me. I just couldn't become that. I wanted to be the girl he wanted, too, but somehow, I was always falling short.

It started with what I ate. When I would sit with Adam, which was nearly every day, he would loudly wonder why I ate different things. If I purchased a bag of chips to go with my sandwich, Adam would question why I was eating junk food. On pizza days, he asked why I didn't opt for the salad. When I got the salad, thinking I was making the safest choice, Adam criticized my choice of fattening dressing. Meanwhile, he would "fuel" his own body with chips and carbs, saying he needed the energy to burn during practice and team lifts.

I know Adam was right about my nutrition, but the pressure to make correct choices in the lunchroom became too much to bear. Ultimately, I began opting to skip lunch all together, usually snacking on an apple rather than braving the temptations in the lunch line. Adam never criticized my lack of lunch, and I decided this was the safest option moving forward. I was happy that I had finally found a solution he seemed to support. After several weeks, my body grew used to the smaller portions and I wasn't even hungry anymore.

On the few days I would eat with Amanda, she would harp on

my lack of lunch, which was just as stressful.

"You're starving yourself," she told me one afternoon. "No one can survive on only an apple every day."

"I eat more than just an apple, Amanda," I grumbled. I was tired of having this conversation. Although I only ate an apple throughout the school day, I was still eating dinner almost every night. I justified there was nothing unhealthy about having fresh fruit for lunch. I even played the "an apple a day keeps the doctor at bay" card on more than one occasion.

"You look like you're wasting away," Amanda huffed one afternoon. In truth, I'd lost over fifteen pounds in the time Adam and I had been dating. He discouraged me from eating snacks, and having an apple every day for lunch was really making a difference. Most of my clothes were fitting looser, and I thought that meant I was healthier than ever before.

"I think she looks great!" Adam was suddenly behind me, his hands resting on my shoulders. He squeezed them slightly, his strong fingers curling around my delicate collar bones. I could feel the heat of his body against my back. Amanda glared at him over my head.

"Good thing no one asked you," Amanda said in the icy tone she seemed to reserve only for Adam.

"You could probably learn a thing or two from Sasha's weight loss," Adam smirked, tilting his head toward the large basket of tater tots in front of Amanda.

On the rare occasions Amanda and Adam spoke, it always felt like I was caught between two warring countries.

"You wouldn't be able to handle these curves." Amanda was never shy about her weight. The fact she was a bigger girl rarely bothered her, and she never let anyone see when it did. Regardless, I didn't like the idea of Adam trying to insult her.

I stood before Adam could say anything else and led him away from the table, shooting a warning look at my best friend in the process.

"Don't be mean to her, Adam," I pleaded as we walked away.

"Mean to her? I was simply trying to stand up for you. She was being mean to you!"

"What? No, she wasn't. She's just concerned." I tried to think back to what Adam might have overheard that he could have misconstrued for cruelty. Amanda was my best friend. She was never mean to me.

"Oh, Sasha, babe, that's why Amanda hates me so much. She hates the fact I stand up for you and don't let her treat you like her little puppet anymore. She's been manipulating you for so long, you don't even see it."

I stopped walking, and Adam leaned against the set of lockers closest to us. Surely Amanda was not manipulating me. We'd been best friends for over a decade. But she did hate Adam, that couldn't be denied.

"She can't even be happy for you when you succeed at something. She's always attempting to bring you down. You lose a little weight and start to look better, and she tears you down. She's jealous of you, and she doesn't want to see you happy."

I couldn't imagine a world where Amanda was jealous of me. But admittedly, she hadn't been very supportive for the past few months. She hadn't been happy for me when I got my first boyfriend, and she'd made it perfectly clear she didn't want to hear about anything that had to do with him. And she was being awfully negative about my weight loss. Maybe Adam was right.

"I guess I never thought about it that way." Suddenly, so many thoughts were racing through my head, I couldn't quite think straight. Was Amanda really jealous of me and therefore trying to sabotage my happiness? How could I not have seen this before? How long had this been going on? How could I possibly have missed it? I thought of how excited Maura had been when I'd told her about Adam and how different Amanda's reaction had been.

Adam leaned forward and kissed me on the forehead.

"It's okay, Sash. I'm here for you. I'm not going to let her take advantage of you anymore."

He wrapped me in a hug before sending me off in the direction of my last class. There were so many thoughts bouncing around in my brain, I never even took out my notebook. I couldn't believe I could be so blind, but now that Adam had pointed it out, I was starting to see how obvious Amanda's jealousy was.

The more I thought about it, the angrier I became. After class, I marched down to the auditorium. I found Amanda in the hallway that led to the costume storage room. She was holding up a hideous purple dress that reminded me of a circus tent.

"Oh, good, Sasha. Don't you agree I can't wear this? It'll make me look ridiculous."

"Why are you so jealous?" I practically yelled the words. I hadn't meant to, but the anger all bubbled to the surface at once when I saw her. I'm not sure who was more surprised, Amanda or myself.

"What the hell are you talking about, Sasha? You're totally out of your mind." Amanda held the dress up and turned back toward the mirror. Her dismissal of my statement made my anger flare up again.

"You're jealous that I have a boyfriend. You're jealous because I'm happy. You're jealous and you've been a total bitch about it for months." Tears were threatening, but I refused to let them come. I didn't want to seem like the same weak little Sasha that Amanda had always been able to manipulate. I wanted to be stronger this time. I wanted Amanda to know she couldn't treat me like that anymore.

Amanda turned toward me, and I watched as her face fought through a variety of emotions. Finally, she laughed. It wasn't the cheery, deep-hearted laugh I was used to. This one was cold and cruel.

"You've got a lot of fucking nerve," Amanda said in almost a whisper. "I don't know what that asshole has been feeding you for lines, but you have no idea what you're saying. And you know something? I don't even care anymore. I'm done. If you want to ruin your life, go right ahead and do it." Amanda marched down the hall, dragging the circus tent behind her.

My chest was heaving as I turned on my heel and stormed off in the opposite direction. It wasn't until I was safely in the bathroom at the other end of the school that I let the tears come. Adam was right. I couldn't believe I'd been so stupid.

CHAPTER TWENTY-FIVE

Adam comforted me over the phone later that night after I told him about my argument with Amanda. He told me not to blame myself for falling for Amanda's manipulation.

"She was being selfish," he said in a calm, soothing voice. "She was used to being able to control you, and she didn't like that I was stopping her from doing that."

I sniffed, trying not to cry anymore. I didn't want Adam to think I was pathetic. I was, but I didn't need to prove it.

I cradled the phone and tried not to think about Amanda anymore. I focused my attention on what Adam was saying. He was concerned about a math test he had coming up. He was taking an algebra course I'd taken two years earlier. He simply didn't understand the material, he claimed. He blamed the teacher, Ms. Thompson, saying she just wasn't explaining the concepts in enough detail.

"I had Ms. Thompson when I took that class. I always thought she was a very good teacher."

"You've already taken this class? Too bad you don't still have your stuff. Imagine how much easier that would be."

"Actually, I keep all my coursework." As the words left my mouth, my cheeks got hot. I knew it was an incredibly nerdy thing to do, but I liked having my previous work to reference.

"Wait, you keep your work from classes you've already taken? So you have this test! It's probably almost exactly the same. I bet she barely changes anything."

"Well, yeah, I suppose I probably have the test."

"That's perfect! I'll study your test and that way I'll know what to expect." Suddenly, I realized what Adam was implying. Panic flooded through me.

"Oh, I don't know. That sounds kind of like cheating." I'd always been an extremely honest student. I wouldn't even check the answer key in the back of the textbook while working on my homework.

"Oh, come on, Sasha, it's not cheating! Cheating would be if I asked you to take the test for me. I'm just asking you to help me study."

Although Adam might have been right, it still felt wrong. I didn't want to be the reason Adam had an unfair advantage on an exam that his classmates wouldn't have. I was quiet as Adam continued to justify why he needed to see my test. It wasn't fair of me to withhold it from him, he argued. He said it was as if I were punishing him for not being as smart as I was.

When I was still hesitant, Adam's voice grew desperate.

"Jesus, Sasha, don't you care about me at all? If I fail this test, I probably won't make the grade cut-off for preseason. I thought you cared about me."

"Of course I care about you!" The panicky feeling was growing stronger. I did care about Adam, and I wanted him to succeed. I was being selfish, I realized. Adam was simply asking for my help. It wasn't really cheating, after all. I was being ridiculous.

"Okay, okay. I'll look through my things and bring the test for you tomorrow."

"You're the best! I'm so lucky to have you." Adam kept talking about how smart I was and how helpful it was that I had already taken most of the classes he was taking right now. While he chattered, I couldn't help but focus on what he had just said. He was lucky to have me? I'd never considered this before. I always thought of myself as the lucky one.

In the months we had been dating, I never felt like I brought much to the table of our relationship. But here I was, a nerdy, social nothing, and Adam felt lucky to have me.

I know, I know, this all sounds so stupid to you, and you're probably thinking about how naïve I am again. Surely you've seen the pattern that emerges when Adam needs help with keeping his grades up. You've probably written "naïve" down in your little notebook a dozen times by now already. I'm sure you're equally amazed by the fact that I was so stupid I didn't see it for myself. Some genius I am.

I guess I can't offer any good excuses. I simply wanted to make Adam happy. I believed I was helping him in the same way any girlfriend would help their boyfriend. I believed Adam would do the same for me. It was the least I could do, I reasoned with myself, since Adam had already been looking out for me.

Adam got an A- on his math test. He was so proud of himself and so excited for the upcoming baseball season. I told myself helping him achieve that couldn't possibly be wrong. He told everyone I was his motivation to do better in school and that I was going to help him get his grades back on track.

His parents were especially proud of Adam's recent academic achievements, and they never seemed to mind when I came over to help Adam study. If only those study sessions had actually involved studying, we both might have been doing better in school.

I'd let Adam convince me to give him my binders for each of the classes he was taking. He told me he studied from my notes, though I think deep down I knew he was simply memorizing my test answers. I was finding it more difficult to keep up with my previously rigorous study schedule. I was spending most evenings and weekends with Adam, which left little time to do much more than my required homework.

One Friday night, I told Adam that I couldn't hang out with him because I needed to catch up on studying for my American History class. I sent the message in response to him texting he would pick me up at eight for a party.

His text messages came rapidly without waiting for any type of response in between.

what the hell kind of an excuse is that??

do u have plans with some other guy tonight???

no one studies on friday night, Sasha

i can't believe ur cheating on me

I tried to convince him I wasn't cheating on him, but he refused to believe me. His messages were angry, and he didn't relent until I agreed to go to the party instead of staying home. I felt defeated, but there was no use arguing with him. I didn't want him to believe I didn't love him.

I told myself Adam was right; no one else was staying home on Friday nights. With Adam, I suddenly had a social life. We went to parties and bonfires and hung out at the mall. There always seemed to be something going on.

My mother encouraged me to go out and never said no when I asked if I could spend time with Adam.

"You're so lucky to have such a sweet boyfriend who includes you in his plans," my mother said when Adam pulled up in front of the house to pick me up for the party. She swooned at every mention of Adam's name. Sometimes I wondered if she was more in love with him than I was.

She offered unsolicited advice constantly on ways to keep Adam happy. She considered herself an expert on the subject.

Don't keep him waiting. Don't complain too much. Don't eat like a slob. Don't be high-maintenance. I could barely keep all her rules straight in my head.

I think she felt like I was finally living up to the standards she'd set when she was a high-school student. Although I was never going to be the captain of the cheerleading squad, at least I was dating a varsity star. In her book, that was socially acceptable. She was content with my place on the high school popularity charts, even if it was only as an accessory.

Life was just so different. Adam and I were practically attached at the hip. I went everywhere he went, did everything he did. If I wasn't physically with Adam, I was texting with him. He always seemed to want to know where I was and what I was doing. I found myself checking in with him almost hourly sometimes. He'd ask for pictures of the places I went, even if it was just the dentist's office. It was as if he needed proof that I was where I said I was.

The first time he asked for a picture of where I was, I questioned him. He told me he wanted to make sure I was safe. It seemed so logical when he said it, and I was flattered by how much he cared about me.

It didn't occur to me there was no plausible way for Adam to determine my safety based on the pictures he'd requested. I just accepted this was something all boyfriends did. It was another part of being in a relationship I just didn't have any experience with. I remember even being thankful Adam was so patient with me as I learned the ropes of being a good girlfriend.

I can imagine what you're thinking now, Doc. The pathetic-ness of it all just keeps building up, doesn't it? But you have to believe me when I say I didn't know any better. Looking back on it now, I guess I can see how strange the whole thing was. But at the time, I trusted him. I believed him. I wanted to make him happy.

Adam got upset so easily, and it always seemed like it was my fault. I was just trying my best. It was never good enough, though. Nothing I did was ever good enough. It seemed like I was always messing things up.

CHAPTER TWENTY-SIX

By the end of February, it was already starting to feel like summer. By late afternoon, the sun would be strong enough to warm your skin, and as long as there was no breeze, you wouldn't even need a jacket. I loved this time of year, where your wardrobe consisted of everything from sweatshirts to tank tops all on the same day.

The baseball team was ready to start practicing outside after school, attempting to gear up for their season as early as possible. Adam was ecstatic on the first day of outdoor practice, and as he drove me to school that day, he animatedly listed off all his personal goals for the upcoming season.

As he parked his truck in the school lot, he was explaining his plan to break the school's home-run record this year.

"If I break the record early enough in the season, there will still be time for scouts to come watch me play before the season ends," Adam explained. I didn't know what the school home-run record was, but Adam was convinced he could surpass it.

His teammates were just as excited about the unofficial start to their season. In the hallway outside of the gym, a group of them chatted about whether other teams were going to be taking advantage of the early spring weather.

"Campton's field is still half underwater from that rainstorm last week," Tony was saying as we joined the group. "There's no way they'll be able to get any practice in until next week at the earliest."

"Too bad," Adam said. "Campton needs all the practice they can get!"

While the players argued about practice strategies, I picked at a string on the sleeve of Adam's sweatshirt. I'd taken to wearing it to school every morning as a jacket. Although it no longer smelled like Adam's cologne, I loved the way it wrapped me in a layer of protection from the high-school food chain. As long as I was wearing Adam's sweatshirt, I was not fair game for bullies that sought out the loners and the weak links.

When the bell rang, Adam slid his hand around my waist and moved me in the direction of my first class. Outside the door, he kissed me quickly and then hurried down the hallway to catch up with Tony and Miles.

Class had barely started when the phone near the door beeped. From across the room, Mr. Adams instructed a student who sat near the phone to answer it. The phone was a direct line of communication to the school's main office. It was rarely used, and even more rarely used for good news.

Mary reached for the phone with an air of importance. After saying hello, she said nothing else before hanging up.

"Is there a Sasha in this class?" Mary asked, looking blankly around the room. Mary was the captain of the varsity volleyball team. She was tall and lean, and her long, silky ponytail swished back and forth as she scanned our classmates.

I awkwardly raised my hand a few inches off my desk. Mary and I had been in many of the same classes since middle school, but I couldn't think of a time we'd ever said two words to each other. We didn't exactly run in similar social circles. But I would have liked to believe she at least knew my name. I was, after all, the only Sasha in the whole school.

Mary shrugged, clearly unfazed by the fact she didn't know me.

"The office wants you," she said as she dropped back into her chair.

I looked toward Mr. Adams, who waved a hand at me from where he was working with a small group of students. Since I hadn't even bothered to open my backpack yet, it wasn't very difficult to gather my belongings. I swung my backpack over my shoulder and tried to slip out of the classroom without drawing any more attention to myself. I tried not to wonder how many of my other classmates were also just now realizing there was a girl named Sasha in their class.

It always amazed me how large the hallways felt when they weren't teeming with students. Sometimes getting to class felt like being in a herd of cattle. But once the bell rang and the students were all required to be elsewhere, the long corridors were abandoned. I tiptoed down the hall, trying to avoid the echo of my sneakers striking the tile.

I'd never been called to the office during class before. I associated being called to the office as something that happened to troublemakers. I knew there was nothing I'd done wrong that would land me in the office, but my mind jumped to fears of being set up or wrongly accused. What if someone claimed I'd done something I hadn't?

As I pushed through the doors of the main office, I was already prepared to defend my innocence against whatever I was being blamed for. I was so caught up in my internal monologue about injustices, I almost walked right into my mother on the other side of the door.

If my mother was here, whatever I'd supposedly done wrong

must be really bad. I was just about to completely panic when I noticed my mother was crying.

Instinctively, I reached for her. She pulled me tight against her, and I could feel her chest heaving with silent sobs. I let her hold me, but my mind was spinning out of control. When I couldn't take not knowing any longer, I pulled away from her embrace and looked at her face.

Her eyes were swollen and red, and her face was blotchy. She hadn't finished doing her hair, and she wasn't wearing any makeup. She shook her head and swallowed.

"Sweetheart, it's Grandma June." She choked on the words, and her tears started fresh. In that moment, I knew there was no point in asking if Grandma June was okay. I knew when we left the school, we wouldn't be going to see her.

My mother pulled me into another hug and sobbed into my neck. Her breath was hot on my skin, and the neckline of my shirt soaked up her tears. I stared over her shoulder at the mailboxes lining the far wall of the office. I processed through the little bit of information I knew, unable to make it sink into my mind.

When my mother pulled away from me, she took my hand and silently led me out of the school. In the car, she managed to explain through giant sobs that Grandma June had been found dead early that morning.

"Probably a heart attack," my mother said.

She told me Grandma June had been carrying a bag of groceries into the house. It must have been dark when it happened. No one noticed her lying on the walkway until this morning, when an early dog walker happened across her.

The tears didn't come until I pictured my poor Grandma June lying on her front walk all night without anyone even knowing she was there. I imagined her lying there, alone, hoping someone would come to her rescue.

I spent the rest of the day sitting at the kitchen table with my mother. We sipped tea and looked through boxes of photos. Between sobs, my mother told me stories about growing up in Grandma June's house. By dinner, there was a mound of used tissues between us and we were both exhausted.

It was still light out when I dragged myself toward my bedroom. I felt like I hadn't slept in days even though it had barely been twelve hours since I'd left my bed.

In my room, I tapped on my cell phone for the first time since leaving the school. I had eighteen text messages from Adam. The first ones started right after first period was over.

hey u werent in ur classroom when i came by

where'd u go??

sasha, why weren't u in ur classroom?

There were a few more after second period that were roughly the same. Adam hadn't been able to find me in the stream of students filing out of my English class.

During third period chem, Adam sent several more messages.

where r u??

why arent u in class??

wtf sasha we're doing a lab today

ur supposed to be here to help me and now i have to do the whole thing by myself

i can't believe u ditched class without telling me

Where the hell did u go?

WTF

Adam's anger seemed to have peaked during chemistry. After that, there was only two messages.

i hope u had fun ditching school

get ur own ride home

I stared at the messages and almost laughed. After everything I'd been through today, Adam's anger about a few missed classes seemed absolutely ridiculous.

I was too tired to be upset with Adam. Instead, I sent him a text message explaining what had happened.

u should have told me

I stared at Adam's response, too drained to answer. In all honesty, it hadn't crossed my mind to tell Adam about Grandma June's death. He hadn't met her, though I had talked about her many times. I didn't think he would care about her passing. But I suppose, it makes sense to tell your boyfriend about these significant events.

I apologized to Adam for not telling him sooner. I apologized to him, and he told me it was okay. Can you believe that? Looking back on it now, I can't believe he didn't apologize to me. My grandmother died! He had no right to be mad at me! But as I always did, I apologized. My grandmother would not have approved.

Grandma June hadn't wanted a big funeral. She left explicit instructions on how to handle her passing, right down to what she wanted written in the paper about her life. It was simple, but fitting. Grandma June had never been a religious woman, and she hated stuffy, morbid affairs. Instead of the usual wake and funeral, Grandma June requested her loved ones gather in the park and read a poem she'd already picked out as a final farewell.

My mother wasn't thrilled with the idea, but in the end, I convinced her to follow Grandma June's last wishes. The Sunday after her passing, my mother and I went to the park and found a sunny spot overlooking the river. We set a large photo of Grandma

June on a nearby park bench and sat silently watching the sunlight dancing on the water. A few people I recognized as Grandma June or my mother's friends gathered around. At three-thirty, my mother patted my knee and welcomed the small crowd, standing behind the park bench that held my grandmother's picture.

After my mother finished, she motioned for me to join her. I hadn't wanted to be the one to read the poem, but my mother insisted. She told me Grandma June would have wanted it this way. I shuffled my feet against the gravel walkway and tried not to make eye contact with anyone in the small group surrounding me.

Focusing on the paper I held in front of me, I read the poem in a shaky voice.

"When I come to the end of the road

And the sun has set for me

I want no rites in a gloom filled room

Why cry for a soul set free?

Miss me a little, but not for long

And not with your head bowed low

Remember the love that once we shared

Miss me, but let me go.

For this is a journey we all must take

And each must go alone.

It's all part of the master plan

A step on the road to home.

When you are lonely and sick at heart

Go to the friends we know.

Laugh at all the things we used to do

Miss me, but let me go."

I memorized the poem over the last few days, making sure I knew every line by heart. I was glad I'd taken the time to get to know it, since before I finished reading the first stanza, my eyes were too filled with tears to focus.

When I finished reading, I made a fuss out of folding up the piece of paper in order to give myself time to recover from the tears. Friends rushed forward and began engulfing my mother and me in weepy hugs. Through my tears and the small crowd, I thought I caught a glimpse of Amanda walking down the path toward the parking lot.

My heart lifted ever so slightly, but by the time I broke away from the other mourners, the girl was gone. I reminded myself that Amanda and I weren't friends anymore and there was no way the girl I saw was her.

That night, lying alone in my bedroom, I cried for a long time. I told myself I was crying because my grandmother had just died, but the truth is, I think it was more than that. I think I was crying because it felt like my world had just gotten a little bit smaller and a whole lot darker.

CHAPTER TWENTY-SEVEN

To be honest, I hadn't wanted Adam at Grandma June's memorial service. I knew I would be emotional, and I didn't want to feel like I needed to hide that from him. Since he'd never met Grandma June, I didn't imagine he would care about the service.

I was surprised when he was offended at the idea of missing it. He argued it was his job to support me in times of need and if I didn't allow him to attend, everyone would assume he was a bad boyfriend. In the end, I managed to convince him to stay home, but he insisted I call him if I felt like I needed him.

When he picked me up for school Monday morning, he brought me a long-stem red rose. He gave me a hug across the center console and kissed me multiple times on the forehead.

"I'm here for you," he said as he pulled the truck away from the curb.

I nodded, allowing myself to take comfort in Adam's support. Instead of standing with his teammates when we arrived at school, Adam led me down the hall toward my first class. We stood together outside of the classroom door, his arms securely wrapped around my waist.

It was nice to feel like I had Adam all to myself in the hallways. I spent the majority of my time as an accessory to Adam's life, like something he brought with him in case he needed it. I would often think of the gigantic purse Amanda would lug around the mall with us. She kept scissors and pens and Chapstick and even pepper spray in that bag. There was never a need for any of those things, but she carried it around everywhere she went just in case. I probably wasn't as useful to Adam as Amanda's purse, but I went everywhere with him anyway.

Standing in the hallway that morning, I felt like I was the only person in Adam's world. I carried the rose he'd given me in my hand, delicately holding it at my side so it wouldn't get crushed or destroyed in the busy halls. Adam fussed over how I was feeling and whether I was all right. I kept assuring him I was fine, but I didn't dislike the attention.

When the bell rang, he kissed me gently and watched me disappear into my classroom. Sitting at my desk, I couldn't help but feel a little guilty that I was enjoying his sympathy. Did that make me a bad person? I wondered if I was somehow disrespecting my Grandma June's memory. Was I taking advantage of the situation?

Adam was so sweet over the next few days that it made me feel even guiltier. I found myself wondering if this was how our relationship could always be if I wasn't constantly making Adam so upset. The entire week following my Grandma's service passed with blissful peace. Adam escorted me around like I was the delicate rose that needed protecting in the crowded hallways. He catered to my every need, jumping up to get me a drink while we were studying and opening the door to his truck for me like my hands were broken. He didn't even say a word when I ordered a slice of pizza for lunch one day.

I probably should have known it was only a matter of time before I messed something up and snapped the spell. A week after Grandma June's service, I'd fallen asleep without plugging my cell phone in to charge. I woke up surrounded by textbooks and homework I'd been trying to finish late the night before. I was quickly starting to fall behind on my work, and I was staying up late into the night attempting to catch up.

I barely had enough time to get ready before Adam pulled into my driveway. After I climbed into the cab of his truck, I checked my phone and realized it only had twelve percent battery left. I told Adam I'd forgotten to charge my phone. He nodded, though he never stopped singing along to the song playing on the radio.

When we arrived at school, Adam led me to my first class as he had done the week before. We stood together outside the classroom, and he gently stroked my cheek with his thumb.

"I'm going to miss you today," he said. Adam was going on a school-sponsored college visit. He was taking a bus to one of the local state universities and getting a tour. Adam told me he couldn't care less about the school itself; he just wanted an excuse to get out of class for the day. He wouldn't get back until just before the final bell rang.

"You'll be having too much fun to miss me," I teased.

"Well, maybe," he said with a grin. The bell rang, and students started rushing toward classroom doors. Adam kissed my forehead and watched me enter the room. He gave a little wave as I took my seat and then headed down the hall in the opposite direction.

Adam sent me a heart emoji a little while later. I assumed he'd just gotten on the bus for the visit. I responded with an emoji and then noticed the little battery on the top of my phone was blinking. I couldn't believe twelve percent of battery had drained so quickly.

I had just started to type out a message telling him my phone was about to die when the screen went dark. I slumped into my chair, annoyed at myself for not plugging my phone in when I had the chance. I slipped the dead device into my backpack and tried to focus on the teacher's lecture.

The day passed slowly without the ability to text with Adam. By lunch, I was feeling truly disconnected. When I entered the lunchroom, I realized the predicament I was in.

Adam wasn't here, which meant I didn't have to sit at his lunch table. In fact, I didn't think I should sit there without him. However, I was no longer speaking to Amanda, so I couldn't sit at my old table either. I stared around the lunchroom, searching for another option. Panic engulfed me as I realized I had nowhere to sit. Without Adam, I was lost.

I retreated out of the lunchroom and walked aimlessly through the hallways. A few other students roamed around, but no one acknowledged me. As I walked, I dug my dead cell phone out of my bag. I pressed the power button, hoping that maybe there was enough power conserved in the battery to give me a few minutes of text time. The screen stayed dark, and I tossed it back into my bag with a sigh.

After what felt like ages, the bell finally rang, ending the lunch period, and I wandered toward my final class. I was looking forward to the end of the school day when I would get to see Adam. I'd already decided I wasn't going to mention to him that I hadn't had anywhere to sit at lunch. I didn't want to remind him how much of a loser I was when he wasn't around.

When school finally ended, I raced out of my classroom, expecting to find Adam waiting right outside my door. I was filled with disappointment when I couldn't immediately find him. I followed the herd of students down the hallway, where I spotted Adam standing among a collection of other baseball players.

I slid through the crowd until I was standing beside him. I expected him to wrap his arm around me, but his attention was focused on the heated discussion he was having with Miles.

After a while, I hesitantly placed my hand on Adam's arm. I was tired of waiting to be acknowledged, and after my long and lonely day, I was desperate for some attention. Adam shot me a warning look, and I quickly withdrew my hand. I huddled behind him for another few minutes, until finally he said goodbye to Miles and the rest of his friends. Without even glancing at me, he started walking toward his truck.

"Hey, wait," I said, as I scurried along behind him. "I've been dying to see you all day." Adam stopped walking and spun toward me with such force it stopped me in my tracks.

"Oh yeah?" he spat. "Is that why you've been ignoring me all day?"

"I wasn't ignoring you! My phone died. I forgot to charge it last night, remember? It died during first period!"

Adam stiffly crossed his arms. The gesture always made him look even larger than he was.

"Why didn't you tell me your phone was dying? I spent all day worried about you."

"I told you this morning! I told you it was only at twelve percent when I woke up." I reached for him, and he allowed me to uncross his arms. I stepped into his body, wrapping my arms around his waist. He let his arms hang loosely at his sides.

"If you had told me that, I would have remembered. You're so goddamn careless. How could you forget to charge your phone?"

I nodded my head against his chest, apologizing for my mistake. Adam eventually wrapped his arms around me, and although he never said it, I took this as a sign of forgiveness. When Adam dropped me off at my house later that afternoon, I thought maybe he had forgotten about the whole thing. But as I walked toward my door, Adam rolled the window down and yelled, "Plug your damn phone in!" before driving off.

CHAPTER TWENTY-EIGHT

Adam liked to be in bed early the night before a game. On the Friday before his first game, I left his house promptly at eight-thirty p.m. It was only a preseason game, but I knew better by now than to assume that made it any less important. He wrapped his arms around me and pulled me close as he kissed me goodbye.

"You're going to be there tomorrow, right?" he whispered into my hair.

"Of course I will be; I'm your biggest fan!" I smiled, letting him lean into me as he kissed my neck.

"Four o'clock," he said. "Don't be late."

When I arrived at the field at ten till four, it looked like the game had already started. I glanced down at my watch before I hefted my camera case out of the backseat of my mom's car. She honked as she drove away and yelled "Go Baymont!" out the window. I ducked my head in embarrassment and hoped no one recognized her as I headed toward the bleachers next to the home team's dugout.

"There you are!" someone called from the stands. "I was

wondering where you were." Melissa Potter was smiling at me from the second row. I slid into the empty spot in front of her and began unpacking my camera. "You missed it! Adam stole home on a pitch to give us the lead last inning!"

"I thought the game started at four," I said as I searched the bodies in the dugout for Adam. I found him leaning against the fence near the end, his catching shin pads on even though his team was up to bat. It felt like he was staring right at me, but when I raised my hand to wave, he didn't move to acknowledge me.

"No," Melissa said, "it was a three o'clock start." She clapped for something that happened out on the field. The older gentleman sitting next to me whistled so loud I almost jumped out of my seat.

I liked Melissa. She'd always been nice to me. Some of Adam's teammate's girlfriends were not as welcoming, but Melissa was different. I quickly learned that there was a hierarchy even amongst the members of the team. It wasn't enough to simply say you were a member of the baseball team.

The "specialty players," like Adam and the pitchers and the first baseman, were at the top of the ladder. Everyone else fell somewhere underneath, right down to the alternate players who never touched the field. Melissa's boyfriend, Teddy, played right field. I learned that he was important, but not essential, in Adam's mind.

Leaving my camera case at Melissa's feet, I moved around the field to take pictures for the rest of the game. Baymont won by two runs, an exciting last inning, judging by the fan's reactions. After the game, I stood near the backstop waiting for Adam.

He looked angry, despite the fact that his team won and it seemed like he'd played well.

"Hey there, all-star!" I said, preparing to lean over to kiss his cheek. But before I even got the full sentence out, Adam barked at me.

"Where were you?" He dropped the heavy bag bursting with his catching equipment between us, and I had to jump backwards to avoid it landing on my toes.

"You told me the game started at four."

"No, I didn't. Saturday games always start at three. Goddamn it, you never listen. You promised you wouldn't be late!"

It actually surprised me that Adam cared so much about me being at his game, and if I hadn't been so flustered, I might have found that cute. I racked my brain, but I was certain he had told me the game started at four. I tried desperately to think of how I could have mixed that up. No matter how I replayed the conversation from the night before, I couldn't remember it any other way.

"I'm sorry," I said, reaching for him. "I could have sworn you said four."

Adam pulled away from me and hefted his bag over his shoulder. I watched as he stalked off toward the locker room. Unaware anything was wrong, Melissa wandered over to stand with me while we waited for the team to shower and be released by the coach.

After a while, Teddy came out of the locker room, freshly showered and looking happy. He grabbed Melissa around the waist and tipped her back to kiss her squarely on the mouth. She giggled as they pulled apart. Teddy looked at me as if he were surprised to see me.

"You're still here? I thought you would have left with Adam."

"I'm waiting for him to come out. He's my ride home."

A look of concern passed over Teddy's face, and he glanced around the parking lot.

"Adam left a while ago…" His voice trailed off, and I followed his gaze. Sure enough, I didn't see Adam's truck in the parking lot anymore. My mind raced through possible explanations. I couldn't imagine he'd actually left without me, but clearly he was gone. I checked my phone, and I had no missed calls or texts from Adam. I tried calling him, but the call was declined.

Teddy drove me home in his older-than-we-are pickup truck. It was clear Melissa and Teddy weren't used to having company on the bench seat. I watched uncomfortably as his hand moved further and further up Melissa's leg as we drove.

About a mile from my house, I told Teddy he could let me out. I needed some fresh air to clear my head. I slung my camera bag over my shoulder and walked slowly along the road that led to my neighborhood.

I tried calling Adam again, and I'd already texted him several times before we even left the school, but he hadn't responded. The panic rose in the back of my mind with every minute that passed where he hadn't acknowledged my message.

This is it, I thought. *I've fucked everything up now.*

He'll dump me by Monday.

I've ruined everything.

I'm such a fuck up.

How could I possibly forget the game start time?

I tried to imagine what I would tell my mother after Adam broke up with me. She'd be so disappointed in me.

By the time I reached my front door, I'd replayed the night before at least a dozen more times in my mind. I could swear he told me the game was at four o'clock. I'd have bet my life on it. But he obviously knew what time his baseball games started. I must have heard him wrong. Maybe I hadn't been listening very closely, especially since I was concentrating on the feeling of his body against mine.

How could I have been so stupid?

When I hadn't heard from Adam at all on Sunday, I resigned myself to the fact that things were over. I cried myself to sleep on Sunday night, certain that when I arrived at school Monday morning Adam would no longer be a part of my life. I wondered how I would survive in chemistry class for the rest of the school year. How would I be able to face him every day knowing it was my fault we weren't together anymore? How would we work together if he hated me? Would Mr. Carter make an exception to his seating chart policies for such horrible circumstances?

On Monday morning, after a restless night's sleep, I arrived at school with a heavy heart and bags under my eyes. I spotted Adam immediately, standing outside the gymnasium with a few other baseball players. I hesitated, unsure of whether I should walk around to the other entrance. Maybe it would spare me the embarrassment of being dumped in front of a group of Adam's friends.

But before I could decide what to do, Adam caught my eye. He smiled and waved, breaking himself free of the group and jogging over to where I was standing. He bent over and kissed me, and I'm sure I wasn't hiding my surprise.

"You look terrible, babe," he said, brushing my frizzy curls away from my face. "Are you feeling alright?"

He was acting so normal, as if the weekend never happened. I stammered an explanation of not sleeping well. I still couldn't believe Adam wasn't breaking up with me on the spot.

"You study too hard," he said, clearly assuming that was the reason for the bags under my eyes. He took my hand and led me toward the gossiping group like it was any normal day.

I was almost too exhausted to process what was happening. Apparently, I was not about to become the ex-girlfriend of Adam Lincoln.

Maybe I hadn't fucked up quite as badly as I thought.

CHAPTER TWENTY-NINE

I guess this is finally what you've been waiting for. You haven't been tapping your pen on your notebook, and you're writing a lot of stuff down. I glance toward your dumb clock again. The stupid paddle minute hand tells me barely an hour and a half has gone by since you first welcomed me into this tiny office.

It feels like days have passed.

I suddenly realize how thirsty I am, and as if reading my mind, you offer me some water. You lean over toward your desk and pour some water into a cup from a large glass pitcher. The flimsy cup bends in my hands as I take it from you, and some water sloshes over the side. It leaves little spots on the rug between us, and I sit there staring at them for a while.

The spots make me think of those black and white ink splotches. Isn't that a tool that therapists use to test if people are crazy? You show me the image, and if I see the butterfly, I'm okay, but if I see the cat, then I'm headed downhill?

I look around the room, but I don't see any ink splotch cards. I wonder if you're waiting until later to show me those. Maybe that's the final test I have to pass.

Tests.

What will happen with my final exams? I know it's about the time I should be taking them. The old Sasha would already have weeks of studying under her belt. There would be lists and study guides and schedules for making sure I had enough time to study for each individual course. If there was one thing I used to be good at, it was studying.

I can't remember the last time I dedicated myself to studying, though. It seems like it's been forever. Adam was never very interested in studying, even when that was what he invited me over for. Study sessions, he would call them. But every time I went over for study sessions, he never had any books or notebooks out.

Instead, he would move close to me on the couch and run his hands up my legs. He'd lean his face close to my neck and kiss up to my lips.

The first time, I was confused. I asked him if he needed to study for a test or something. He laughed into my hair and told me he was studying biology. I'd be lying if I said I understood why he said that. I knew he wasn't taking biology.

Studying became one of those things that just didn't seem important when Adam and I were together. And since we were together almost all the time, I didn't have nearly enough time to study on my own, so I just didn't.

I can't tell you what my grades are right now, but I imagine they're letters of the alphabet my report cards were not used to seeing. Last semester, when my report card came in the mail, my mother called the school to see if there was some mistake. She said there must have been a computer error. There was no way I was getting so many Cs. And a D in English? Impossible. But the school assured her there was no error. Those were really the grades I had earned.

Well, not really earned. I hadn't earned anything. I pretty much just stopped putting any effort into school all together. But I couldn't tell my mother that. There's no way she would have understood.

You're trying to make it sound like you're just asking a casual question, but I know my answer holds a lot of weight.

"Why did you stop putting effort into school?"

Although it sounds like a simple question, there isn't a simple answer.

Sure, it started because Adam and I didn't have time to study. It's easy to blame my bad grades on that. We were so caught up in each other nothing else seemed to matter.

But then it became more than that.

I didn't see the point anymore. What was the benefit of putting in all that effort? Everything had become so complicated. School was easy. If I didn't want to try, I didn't have to.

So I just stopped trying.

CHAPTER THIRTY

After the debacle with the baseball game, I tried so hard not to screw anything else up. I assumed at this point I was probably running out of chances. I was positive if I continued to make such stupid mistakes, Adam would no longer want to be with me. If Adam broke up with me, what would I have left?

But it seemed like the harder I tried to be the perfect girlfriend, the more I fucked everything up. The whole thing baffled me. How could I be so book smart and remember obscure dates and facts for meaningless tests, but at the same time be so stupid when it came to remembering important details?

On the way to school one morning, Adam asked me to run into the store and buy him a Gatorade while he pumped gas. I asked him what flavor he wanted as I hopped out of the truck. He was looking through his wallet for his credit card to pay for the gas. He shrugged and told me it didn't matter.

I jogged across the gas station parking lot and into the little convenience store that had been managed by the same family for my entire life. Mr. Olsen stood at the counter and greeted me when I came in. He asked about school and my mother and if I was enjoying the nice weather.

After a few minutes, another customer came into the store and drew Mr. Olsen's attention. Seizing the opportunity to break away from his small talk, I quickly went to the back of the store and grabbed a blue Gatorade out of the cooler.

On my way back to the counter, I spotted those cream-filled chocolate eggs that every store sells around Easter time. They're only a quarter each, and I decided to treat myself to one. I slid the candy and the Gatorade onto the counter, and Mr. Olsen rang them up.

"Breakfast of champions," he said with a wink.

I laughed and told him to have a good day. I pushed out the door and hurried across the parking lot. Adam's truck was running, and he was sitting inside, scrolling through his phone.

"Jesus, what took you so long?" he asked as soon as I opened the door.

"Sorry," I said as I climbed inside. "Mr. Olsen was in a talkative mood this morning."

Adam glanced toward the large glass window that dominated the front of the convenience store. Inside, Mr. Olsen was leaning against the counter, talking to someone just out of view. I held out the Gatorade to Adam.

"What is this?" he asked, staring down at the bottle in my hand in disgust. I looked down at it, too.

"Uh, it's your Gatorade." I extended my hand further, as if giving him a closer look at the bottle I was holding might answer his question.

"I asked for a red one. Damnit, Sasha, you never listen."

Adam slammed the truck into drive and accelerated quickly out of the parking lot. I was still holding the Gatorade between us, unsure of what else to do.

"I thought you said it didn't matter what flavor it was," I said, after a long moment of tense silence. I barely whispered the words. I gently slid the Gatorade into the truck's cup holder. I folded into myself in the passenger seat, cradling the chocolate egg in my hands.

"Figures," Adam snarled, "you couldn't bother to listen to what I asked for, but you made sure to get candy for yourself." Adam grabbed the bottle out of the cup holder and threw it onto the floor of the backseat. I heard the bottle rolling around as he turned the truck sharply into the school parking lot. He whipped into a spot, not even bothering to ensure that he was properly in the space.

"I hope you enjoy your chocolate," he growled. Then he slammed the door and stalked toward the school.

I sat there in shocked silence, still holding the foil-wrapped chocolate in my hands. I desperately tried to recall Adam asking me specifically to get him a red Gatorade. Did he say it as I was climbing out of the car? Was his voice drowned out by passing traffic or some other noise? Had he actually asked for that all along and I'd forgotten during my conversation with Mr. Olsen? Or had I really been so distracted by finding my favorite holiday candy I mixed everything up in my head?

I stared down at the candy I was cradling and suddenly couldn't imagine eating it. I slid out of the truck and gathered my backpack. I walked slowly toward the school and dropped the chocolate into the trashcan beside the entrance.

I walked directly to my first classroom, not bothering to detour down to the hallway where Adam would be hanging out with his friends. I knew he wouldn't want to see me right now. I wondered what his friends would think when I didn't appear beside him. Would they know I messed up such a simple favor? Would Adam tell them how useless I was?

Instead of preparing my notebooks for class as I normally would, I took out my phone and began tapping out a message. It took me several tries to find the right wording, but I sent Adam an apology.

I apologized for not listening more closely and for being so stupid. I promised him I would do better and begged him to forgive me. After hitting send, I watched for his response, but it didn't come.

When the bell rang, I slipped my phone into my bag and rested my head in my arms. Ignoring the lecture, I fought back tears throughout the entire class. My mind was completely preoccupied with thoughts of my failure. Adam still hadn't responded to my text by the time chemistry started. I was dreading going to class, positive he would have made up his mind to dump me prior to the period.

I dragged myself into the classroom and perched uneasily on my lab stool. When Adam entered the room, he looked as handsome as ever. He didn't appear weighed down with anger or resentment. He leaned over to kiss me gently on the cheek as he took his seat.

I eyed him cautiously, waiting for him to betray his anger toward me. Instead, Adam dropped his bag onto the floor next to his stool and started to talk about something his coach had just told him. He seemed happy and excited. There was no indication the morning's argument had even happened.

As class continued, I let my shoulders start to relax. I allowed myself to believe Adam had forgiven me and gotten over his anger. Maybe he realized he hadn't asked me for a red Gatorade and I'd been right all along.

With only a few minutes left before the bell rang, Adam leaned across the table so he was only a few inches away from me.

"Where's your chocolate?"

The words were laced with spite. My shoulders tensed and I knew this was to remind me of my earlier mistake. Adam was letting me know he hadn't forgotten at all. The tears stung my eyes.

"I threw it out," I whispered.

My voice caught in my throat and cracked. I swallowed hard as I tried to prevent the tears from spilling over.

Adam leaned back on his stool.

"Good," he said, half smirking. "You didn't need it anyway."

The bell rang and Adam stood, pulling his backpack over one shoulder. He held his hand out to me, and when I placed mine inside it, he squeezed my fingers tightly. Although the gesture was loving, the pressure he was placing on my fingers felt like a punishment. He maintained the pressure all the way to the lunchroom, where he guided me to my seat and waited for me to sit down.

Adam placed his hands firmly on each of my shoulders and squeezed. The pressure made me wince, though I can't say it actually hurt. Even after he walked away, I could still feel his fingers locking around my collarbones.

CHAPTER THIRTY-ONE

I know I sound crazy.

Something as stupid as an argument over the color of a Gatorade is enough to unhinge me. But there were so many things, little things, things that would be insignificant to anyone else.

Sometimes it would seem like simple oversights. Adam would tell me something and I swear it was the first time I'd ever heard it, but he would insist he'd told me dozens of times before.

Then there were the times I could recall the conversation, but I'd remember the details entirely differently than Adam. Similar to the Gatorade color or the time of his baseball game. I would swear he told me one thing, but he was positive I was wrong.

Worse than the Gatorade argument or being late to the baseball game, though, was the day I almost ruined his mother's birthday party.

I really liked Mrs. Lincoln. She always took the time to say hello to me whenever I came over, even though it seemed like she was always busy in the kitchen. She'd step away from the oven and rub her hands with a faded dish cloth while she asked how my day was going. She always seemed interested in my answers, not like other adults who just ask how you're doing to fill space in the conversation. She wanted to hear more than just "fine."

Adam told me her birthday was coming up. I'd gone with him to the mall, and we wandered the stores looking for a gift for her. He ultimately settled on a wooden statue that resembled an angel holding a lantern. He'd been pleased with his purchase and was looking forward to giving the gift to his mother.

I asked him when his mother's birthday was, and I was certain he'd simply responded "next week." Even now, I still feel like I would have remembered if he said the date.

On Friday night, when Adam invited me over, I didn't think there was anything special about the invitation. He said it in the same nonchalant way he did every day, as if the invitation were a formality and it was more of an expectation.

I arrived in the faded blue jeans I'd worn to school. They had a hole under the back pocket on the left side. I was convinced they were trendy, and I liked the way they looked, but I wouldn't call them formal by any stretch of the imagination. I paired them with a plain green tee shirt and threw my hair on top of my head in a messy bun. Adam hadn't mentioned any of his friends having parties this weekend, so I anticipated we'd just be hanging out and watching a movie.

What I was certainly not prepared for was Adam answering the door in his nicest khaki pants, a white button-down shirt, and a baby blue tie. I watched his face transform into a look of pure disgust at the sight of me.

"What are you wearing?" He glanced down the hallway toward the living room. I looked down at my tee shirt and torn jeans. I searched my brain for an explanation as to why he was dressed up, but I couldn't think of anything. I nervously smoothed my tee shirt with my palms.

"This is just what I had on at school. I, uh, was I supposed to wear something else?" I stammered over the words. I could already tell from his face I was supposed to be wearing something else, but I had no idea why or what that was supposed to be.

"It's my mother's goddamn birthday! You couldn't find something more appropriate to wear to the restaurant?" He spit the words through a clenched jaw. The muscles in his neck strained with anger. I was completely dumbfounded.

"Today? Restaurant? I didn't know—you didn't say, oh my God, I'm so sorry."

I fumbled for some sort of explanation, but Adam was only getting angrier.

"We're supposed to be leaving in five minutes. Everyone's hungry, and we've been waiting for you to get here, and this is how you show up? I can't believe you right now." He was seething with anger. I had no idea what to do.

"I'll run home and change. I'll be right back. I'll fix it."

"Forget it, Sasha; it's too late now. You'll have to just go like that, looking like trash." He turned on his heel and walked down the hall toward the living room, leaving me standing in the doorway.

I was mortified. How could I have forgotten Adam's mother's birthday? Surely if he told me we were going out to a fancy dinner, I would have remembered. I would have stopped to pick up flowers for Mrs. Lincoln. I would have worn my nice black pants and my new sweater. I considered just running to my mother's car and driving home. Was it worse to disappear altogether?

I slunk down the hallway toward the voices of Adam's parents. Adam stood in the entryway, his arms crossed against his chest. His annoyance was palpable. I shyly stood at his elbow, looking down at the floor.

"Hello, Sasha, dear," Mrs. Lincoln said as soon as I entered the room. She crossed the room and draped me in a sincere hug. She was wearing a tea-length black dress with a pair of simple heels. She looked classic and elegant. The sight of her made me feel even more guilty.

"Happy Birthday, Mrs. Lincoln. I'm so sorry, I didn't realize we were going out to dinner to celebrate. I would have worn something more appropriate." My voice cracked as I said the words, and the tears were gathering in my throat.

Mrs. Lincoln waved her hand, brushing away my apology.

"You look lovely," she said, though I knew she was lying. I stared down at the toes of my faded and dirty sneakers, aware that everyone else's shoes were shining in the living room light. Mr. Lincoln cleared his throat and looked up from his phone.

"Well, if we're going to make our reservation, we need to leave now. But the restaurant does have a dress code. There's no jeans allowed. Sasha, I'm sorry, but you won't be able to come with us."

I opened my mouth to apologize further, to tell the Lincolns that of course, I understood why I couldn't come to dinner with them and they should go and have a wonderful time. But before I could say any of that, Mrs. Lincoln cut me off.

"Nonsense," she said, her hands on her hips. "If Sasha can't go with us, then we'll go somewhere else."

I stared at Mrs. Lincoln, my mouth still open from my attempt to apologize. Adam and his father were both staring at her, too.

"Honey," Mr. Lincoln said through tight lips, "I made this reservation months ago. You've been looking forward to it all this time." Mr. Lincoln glanced at me, and I could see the same muscles working in his jaw that I was used to seeing in Adam. At this moment, it was almost hard to tell them apart.

"Don't let me ruin your plans, Mrs. Lincoln, really. I'm so sorry. You guys go and have fun."

I tried not to look at Adam or his father, though I could feel them both glaring at me. I knew my cheeks were flushing a deep red. I wanted to run from the room. I wanted to disappear. Mrs. Lincoln smiled and stepped out of her heels.

"You're all being ridiculous. Let me run and change and then we'll go and get Chinese." With that, Mrs. Lincoln disappeared down the hall.

Mr. Lincoln followed her. I could hear their voices drifting down the hallway, but I couldn't make out what was being said. Adam hadn't moved, but I could still feel him glaring at me.

"I hope you're happy," he said finally. I was just about to plead with him when his parents emerged from their room. Mrs. Lincoln wore jeans and a cream-colored sweater. She was still smiling warmly as she gathered her purse off a chair near the door. Mr. Lincoln had removed his tie. He was not smiling, but he said nothing else about the ruined reservation.

"Really," I said, trying to apologize one more time, "don't change everything because of me-" Mrs. Lincoln raised her hand to silence me.

"It's my birthday, and I would really enjoy getting some Chinese food," she said, dismissing my final attempt. With that, everyone silently climbed into Mr. Lincoln's car.

Though the drive was tense and silent, Mrs. Lincoln managed to turn her husband and son's moods around at the restaurant. She was such a vibrantly happy woman that it was hard to remain upset in her presence. She raved about her food, and when she finally pushed her bowl away, she declared she could not have eaten a better meal for her birthday.

Later, when I was getting ready to go home, I pulled Mrs. Lincoln aside in the kitchen and tried to apologize to her again. Although it did appear like she'd enjoyed her night, I was still sorry she hadn't gotten the dinner she'd planned to have.

Once again, Mrs. Lincoln waved away my apology.

"These things happen," she said. "We all make mistakes." I wondered if she knew how many mistakes I was making lately.

Adam kissed me goodnight, seemingly having decided to forgive me.

"You sure can be forgetful sometime, Sasha," he said as he walked me to my car. I apologized again and promised to try harder.

But lying in bed that night, I couldn't sleep. I replayed every conversation I could recall regarding Adam's mom and her birthday. I felt so positive he never told me when her birthday was, and he certainly never invited me to celebrate it with them. I told myself there was no way I would have forgotten that.

As the night hours slowly slipped by, I wondered about all the times Adam insisted he told me things I couldn't remember.

Was I really that forgetful?

My mind was telling me no, but what else was I supposed to believe?

CHAPTER THIRTY-TWO

After his mother's birthday, I was trying even harder to pay attention to the things Adam told me. I was even starting to write things down to try and help me remember. Although it still felt like I was missing a lot of little details, I managed to avoid any further big disasters for a while.

I'd been attending all of Adam's games and taking pictures. After each game, I would carefully edit the images and post them to Facebook. His teammates seemed to love seeing the pictures. I thought Adam was thrilled with the quality of my work and how much his friends were enjoying it.

By the halfway point in the season, nearly all of Adam's teammates were using pictures I'd taken as their profile pictures on social media. Adam had been the first one to change his picture. He was currently using a shot I'd taken of him in the first game of the regular season. In it, he's standing over the plate with his mask off, posed to throw down a runner. He looks menacing and imposing, as if he's daring the runner to test his arm. I was very proud of the shot, and I was ecstatic when Adam fell in love with it, too.

Actually, if I'm being honest, I was really enjoying having an audience for my pictures. I'd never shared my work so publicly before. Amanda used to scroll through the images on my camera occasionally. She would tell me they were nice, and she sometimes made suggestions on which one I should submit to a contest, but she wasn't truly interested in photography.

Adam's teammates looked forward to me posting my pictures after each game. Some of them would even message me to ask when I was going to post new albums.

One Friday night after a particularly close game in which Baymont had just barely won, I was sitting on the floor with my laptop in my lap and my back against Adam's couch. Adam sat above me, flicking through channels, trying to find something to watch on TV. He said he was too tired from the game to do anything, but now he seemed restless and bored.

I'd uploaded the raw images I'd taken earlier and I was working on editing my favorite ones. I was concentrating on editing a photo of Baymont's second baseman when my computer dinged with a Facebook notification. I clicked away from my photo editing program and checked my page. I opened the message, which was from one of Adam's teammates, George. George had pitched the start of the game. I had taken some really good pictures of him, and I was excited to share them with him.

New photos tonight?

I responded to the message, promising the photos would be up by the morning. George sent back an image of a thumbs up sign. I closed the message window and returned to editing the photo I'd been working on.

"Why are you messaging with George?" Adam asked. He'd stopped scanning the TV channels and was leaning down toward my screen.

"He was just asking if I was going to post pictures from tonight's game. I told him I would have them posted by the morning."

"But why was he messaging you about it?" Adam reached for my laptop, pulling it off my lap. He clicked back to my Facebook and opened my messages. I didn't talk to many people on Facebook. There were three or four messages just like George's from the last few weeks from other teammates. I'd been flattered to receive each one, always making sure to include an extra photo of anyone who took the time to ask about the pictures.

I hadn't thought anything of the messages, but now, I suddenly wished I'd deleted them. Adam clicked each thread open and read the messages with his face twisted into a scowl.

"Why are you messaging with all my teammates behind my back?" he demanded, after he clicked through each thread multiple times.

"I wasn't doing it behind your back! They were only asking me about the pictures." I tried to grab my laptop back from Adam, but he held it out of my reach.

"What the hell, Sasha! Is this why you're working so hard on that picture of Greg? Cause you're secretly messaging with him?" Adam clicked back to the picture I was working on. I thought it was a great action shot. Greg was in midair, his glove outstretched over his head. The ball was just visible in the webbing. I'd been really happy with my timing.

"What are you talking about, Adam? I'm just editing the pictures the way I always do." I made a second attempt at taking my computer back, but Adam continued to hold it out of my reach.

"If I had known letting you take pictures at my games was going to make you think you could start sneaking around and talking to all my teammates, I never would have allowed it. No more taking pictures! And no more talking to my friends on Facebook! I can't believe you would do that to me."

"Adam! You're being crazy!" I watched in horror as Adam dragged the folder of photos I was working on into the computer's digital trash. I tried again to get my computer away from him, but he turned so his body was blocking it from me. "Adam, stop! What are you doing? Those are my pictures!"

"If you truly loved me, you wouldn't have been taking pictures of all these other guys. And you certainly wouldn't be talking to them behind my back!" He clicked on the trash and permanently deleted the files. He turned and pushed the computer back towards me. "Now go on and block all the guys you've been messaging with behind my back. You shouldn't be talking to any other guys. You're my girlfriend, for Christ's sakes, Sasha. I can't believe you."

I held the computer in my lap, staring at the empty trash folder. He actually deleted all the images. Adam leaned over me and watched as I opened Facebook and blocked each of his teammates. I didn't understand why he was so upset, but I felt like it was easier to just do what he asked. When I was done, Adam snapped my laptop closed and pulled me onto the couch next to him.

"Why do you try so hard to make me angry, Sasha? Don't you want us to be happy?"

My head was spinning. I was so confused. I didn't understand what I'd done wrong or why Adam became so angry. He squeezed his arm around my shoulders.

I apologized, something I was getting increasingly good at. A lot of times I didn't even know what I was saying I was sorry for; I just knew it was better to apologize than to argue. I repeatedly told Adam I was sorry until his grip on my shoulders loosened.

He clicked through the channels for another hour or so in silence before he announced he was tired and was going to bed. I stood and reached for my laptop. Adam grabbed it first and held it out to me. He held onto it as I tried to take it from him. We stood there for a split second, both of us holding on to a side of my computer.

"I love you, Sasha," Adam said.

"I love you, too, Adam." Something in Adam's expression seemed to want me to say more, but I didn't know what. After another moment, Adam dropped his hand from my laptop and watched me secure the computer in my backpack.

"No more pictures," Adam said, as he walked me toward the door. "I think that's best."

"Okay," I said. Again, I didn't understand, but I realized there was no point in arguing. I didn't know why it was best and I didn't bother to ask. Once Adam decided something, there was simply no changing his mind.

CHAPTER THIRTY-THREE

On Saturday night, Adam decided he wanted to go to a party that his friend, John, was throwing. I'd gone with Adam to a few small parties at different teammate's houses, but this was the first time we would be attending a big house party.

As Adam led me inside, I couldn't believe how many kids were packed inside. I didn't even recognize a lot of them. Some were wearing sweatshirts from other school's sports teams, and I wondered how John even knew this many people.

Adam guided me toward the kitchen, which was no less crowded than the living room. A large group huddled around the kitchen table, where a game of flip cup was in full swing. Although I knew the basic idea of the game from various movies, I'd never actually seen it being played. I wanted to watch, but Adam steered me toward the island where various bottles were arranged next to a stack of paper cups.

Tommy Fisher stood next to the bottles, the unofficial guard of the forbidden goods.

"What'll it be, folks?" he asked as Adam handed him a ten-dollar bill. I shook my head, intending to pass on drinking. All the bottles on the counter were hard liquor, and I'd only ever had a few sips of beer. Adam requested a vodka soda for me, and Tommy poured the drink. Adam pressed the plastic cup into my hands even as I tried to refuse it.

"You'll like it," he said, collecting his own plastic cup from Tommy. He paused to write our names on the cups using a black Sharpie. He explained to me that, now that he'd paid for our cups, I could come up and get as many refills as I wanted.

"Don't lose your cup, though. I'm not buying you another."

I followed him back through the crowd into the living room. The music was too loud, and everyone yelled to be heard over the sound. Adam found a few of his teammates, and I stood awkwardly next to him as they discussed the rest of the baseball season. It was the same conversation I'd listened to him have several times with various people. He was taking long swigs from his cup as they argued over who was going to be their toughest competition for the state title.

I took a delicate sip out of my own cup. It burned the inside of my nose as I swallowed it. The hot liquid moved down my throat and landed heavily in my stomach. I tried not to make a face, but I couldn't help it. Adam raised his eyebrows at me over the rim of his own glass. I tried to smile. I didn't want him to think I wasn't grateful for the drink he'd bought me.

Adam was deeply engaged in the argument, insisting that Plainfield would be their biggest competition. They had a transfer student that could throw a nasty curveball. I'd heard him say that so many times recently; I'm not sure if I actually heard him say it out loud or just in my head.

I turned my attention back to my cup. I swirled it in slow circles and watched the thick liquid spin over itself. I was so transfixed by the movement, I almost didn't realize anyone was speaking to me.

When I looked up, John was standing directly in front of me, his head tipped to one side expectantly. My cheeks flushed slightly as I realized he was waiting for me to answer a question that I didn't hear. I fumbled through an apology and blamed the loud music.

"It's okay," he said, "I just asked if you were enjoying yourself."

My cheeks burned. Why did I always manage to make myself look so stupid in front of Adam's friends? They all must think I'm an idiot.

"Oh, yes, I am." Unsure of what else to say, I added, "Thanks for having us all over."

It felt like a stupid thing to say, and I cursed my horrible social skills. John shrugged.

"It's just kind of what you do when your parents are out of town, right? I'm pretty sure my parents know I throw these parties, but they care more about checking vacation spots off their bucket list than they do about supervising me, so fuck them." John shrugged again and sipped from his own cup. I couldn't tell if he was mad or happy to have been left at home. I didn't know John very well, and I wasn't sure if I was expected to continue the conversation.

"Sorry," I said instinctively. "I'm not really used to the party scene."

I looked at all the people surrounding us. As I moved my eyes around the room, I realized that Adam was staring at me. I hadn't noticed him moving away with his teammates, but now he was standing against the far wall, watching me. I smiled, but he didn't return the gesture.

"You'll get used to it," John was saying. He took what must have been the last sip from his cup and tipped it toward me. "Time for a refill. Need anything?" I shook my head and John moved away through the crowd.

I immediately pushed my way over to Adam. When I reached his side, he grabbed my arm and pulled me against him. He planted a kiss on my lips, though it felt more forceful than loving. I could taste the familiar cinnamon spice on his breath again which I now realized was from his preferred brand of liquor.

"Why were you flirting with John?" He said the words directly into my ear. His fingers tighten around my bicep, where he was still holding me close to him.

"I wasn't flirting!" I protested. I tried to pull away to look at him, but Adam held me in place.

"I saw you blushing as you flirted with him."

"No! I... well, I was embarrassed. I didn't know what to say."

Adam kissed me again, roughly. His lips pushed hard against mine, and it almost hurt.

"You're mine," he said into my ear when he finally pulled away. "No one else's." I nodded, fighting back the tears building behind my eyes. Adam draped his arm around my shoulders and kept me tight against his body as he turned his attention back to his friends.

They started a card game I didn't understand. Adam declined joining in, so I did as well. Mark went to the kitchen and refilled Adam's drink while I continued to nurse mine. I took tiny sips, trying to empty the cup without burning the inside of my esophagus.

After a while, Adam took my hand and led me away from the confusing game. He tugged me through the noise and crowd toward the entryway. I was hopeful maybe he'd decided he'd had enough for the night and we were going to leave. The noise in the house was starting to give me a headache, and I could feel my stomach turning over the vodka I'd managed to get down.

But when we reached the entryway, Adam turned away from the front door and led me upstairs instead. I followed him down the hall to a door that had been left partly open. Adam pushed on the door and stood aside so I could enter the room ahead of him.

It appeared to be a guest bedroom. It was painted a deep shade of green, and the bed was covered in bright white blankets. I assumed it was a guest room, because there were no personal touches on any of the walls or shelves. Just a few decorative books and stock photos of beaches. I studied the picture closest to me. It was a generic photo of an Adirondack chair on an empty beach, a large umbrella casting inviting shade over the spot. I knew I would have been able to take a much more creative picture.

I turned back to Adam when I heard him pull the bedroom door closed. I watched him turn the little lock on the door handle, giving us privacy from the party downstairs. I could still hear the noise, but we didn't have to yell to be heard in this room.

I felt a shiver slide down my back as Adam moved toward me. He put his hands on my hips and kissed me, deeply and more gently than before. I wrapped my arms around his neck and kissed him back, happy to be away from the crowd and alone with him.

Adam stepped forward, pushing me toward the bed behind me. When my legs bumped against it, he folded me backwards until I was lying on top of the plush, white comforter. It fluffed around me like a cloud, and for a second, it felt almost magical.

Adam straddled my hips and leaned down to kiss me again. He moved his mouth away from mine and kissed down my cheeks and my neck. He reached the neckline of my tee shirt and paused. His hands slipped under the bottom of my shirt, and my breath caught in my throat. Adam pushed the fabric up so it bunched around my neck, exposing my black lace bra and bare stomach.

He pulled the shirt up over my head and tossed it aside on the bed. I suddenly felt very self-conscious in the bright light of the room. I brought my hands to my chest to try to cover my exposed skin, but Adam moved them away. He sat back on his heels and seemed to be admiring me. Then he leaned down and brushed his lips softly against my skin again. Despite the heat of his breath, goose bumps prickled across my arms and chest.

Adam slid one hand underneath me, and his fingers fumbled with the clasp of my bra. His rough skin scratched at my back as he worked at the closure. I held my breath as he freed the clasp and the bra went loose around me. He pulled the fabric away and tossed it in the direction my tee shirt had gone. I instinctively moved my hands again to cover my now-naked torso, but Adam grabbed my wrists to stop me.

He guided one of my hands toward his crotch. I could feel him harden under my touch, but I didn't know what to do next. I just left my hand where he'd put it as he started roughly squeezing my bare breasts. His hands moved from side to side, squeezing from different angles. I was just starting to wonder if it was supposed to feel good when he suddenly stopped.

Adam shifted over onto one leg, removing his weight from my hips. He reached down and started tugging my skirt up to expose my underwear. He shifted off the bed, popping the button open on his own jeans. He slid the zipper down, and it suddenly dawned on me that Adam didn't plan to stop at second base.

I propped myself up onto my elbows and attempted to pull away from him.

"No, wait," I said. "I don't think I'm ready for this."

Adam's pants were already around his ankles. He was pulling a foil square out of his wallet.

"Why not?" Adam said. There was a slight slur to his words and annoyance in his tone. His eyes looked fierce as he pinned me down with his stare. I looked away from him, searching the bare walls of the room for the appropriate response.

"I…I don't know." I tried to cover myself. I could feel the embarrassment flooding my almost naked body. I looked around, hoping there was a blanket or pillow near enough that I could shield my body with.

"Would you rather fuck John? Should I go get him instead, slut?" Adam spit out the words, and I reeled back like he'd slapped me.

"Of course not!" I felt the tears coming. I tried to blink them away.

"Well then, why not? Don't you love me?" Despite his anger, I thought it sounded like Adam was hurt. I collapsed back onto the bed and raked my hands over my face. This wasn't what I wanted for my first time; it was all wrong. But I didn't want Adam to think I didn't love him.

"Of course I love you. I'm just not sure. I...I don't think I'm ready." My voice cracked as I tried to say the words. Tears rolled down my face, and I swiped them away.

"If you love me, you have to show me," he said.

I watched Adam unroll the condom over himself, and when he climbed on top of me again, I didn't try to move away.

I squeezed my eyes shut as Adam tugged my underwear down. He positioned himself between my legs, and I held my breath as he pushed inside me. I clenched my teeth against the sudden explosion of pain. I told myself I loved Adam over and over again as he moved back and forth above me.

When it was over, Adam pulled off the condom and tossed it into the wastebasket next to the bed. I noticed there were several other foil wrappers inside the trashcan, and I wondered how many other couples used this room for the same purpose.

Adam pulled his pants back up and waited for me to redress myself. I felt the pain between my legs as I stood to straighten my skirt and return my underwear to its proper position. I felt like I'd just done something vile and dirty, and I suddenly wanted nothing more than to go home and take a shower. Adam happily escorted me down the stairs, and I couldn't detect even a trace of anger as we returned to the party.

Once back in the crowd, a few friends gave him high-fives and glanced knowingly in my direction. I crossed my arms over myself, trying to fend off their looks. I told Adam I was tired and wanted to go home.

"I'll bet you're tired," Adam said loudly, eliciting several smirks and another round of high-fives from his friends.

He held my hand on the way home and kissed me gently in front of my house. I could still taste the cinnamon on his breath. He told me he loved me and that he had a wonderful time. I told him I loved him back and slid out of the car.

Alone in my bedroom, I pulled off my underwear. I could see stains of blood on the inside, and the sight of it made me feel sick. I stuffed the underwear into the bottom of the trashcan in the bathroom and took a long shower.

Standing under the water, I allowed more tears to come. I realized after a while I didn't even know why I was crying anymore. After I dried off and got into my pajamas, I sat on my own bed and held my phone. I'd received two messages from Adam while I was in the shower, both telling me how amazing I was.

I opened the thread of texts with Amanda. I realized how long it had been since we'd last spoken. I started typing her a message, but I deleted the words before ever hitting send. I didn't know what it was I wanted to say, anyways.

I climbed into bed and turned out the light. I forced myself not to focus on the dull throbbing between my legs. I told myself it wouldn't always feel like this. I'd heard it only hurt the first time. It took a while, but I was finally able to fall asleep.

CHAPTER THIRTY-FOUR

The word "rape" echoes around the room like a gunshot. I stare at you, certain you must be mistaken. Maybe you haven't been listening this whole time after all. Perhaps you've been doodling on that notepad instead of making notes.

Adam isn't some stranger who pulled me into a dark alley, I argue. I can hear the defensiveness in my tone. I cross my arms tightly over my chest and rock forwards in my chair. You're putting words in my mouth and trying to make Adam into some sort of monster.

Your face softens into something that looks an awful lot like pity.

"Just because Adam was your boyfriend doesn't give him a right to your body without your freely given consent."

I open my mouth to protest on Adam's behalf, but nothing comes out.

You're still talking, using words like "victim" and "sexual assault," but my mind can't process any of it. I replay that night at John's party again in my mind. It didn't feel like rape. It had hurt, but everyone says it's supposed to hurt a little your first time. I compare what happened to the scenes I can remember from various episodes of Law and Order: SVU. He didn't hold me down or tie me up. It wasn't a violent, rage-fueled encounter like Detectives Benson and Stabler investigate day after day on the show.

You remind me I told Adam I didn't want to have sex. That is true. I'd said I didn't want to do it. I hadn't wanted to do it at all. I told Adam I wasn't ready, but I didn't stop him when he pushed inside of me. I didn't scream or fight back. I simply closed my eyes and wished for it to be over.

If I tried harder to stop him, would he have stopped? I wasn't actually sure of the answer.

But he had wanted me to show him that I loved him. I hadn't wanted him to believe I didn't love him. You shake your head and tell me that if he loved me, he would have respected my decision when I said no the first time. I watch as your pen moves across your notepad. I wonder if that's really true.

I'm not a prude. It's not that I didn't ever want to have sex. Amanda and I talked about sex lots of times before. I always imagined my first time would involve candlelight and soft, gentle music. I remember the way the walls seemed to pulse with the bass from the music a floor below us. I felt the bass beating in my temples as I lay on the bed with my skirt around my waist.

You're right, I hadn't wanted to have sex that night. I hadn't wanted that to be my first time. I just hadn't wanted to disappoint Adam. I wonder why he hadn't listened to me when I told him I wasn't ready. Did I tell him clearly enough? Maybe he misunderstood what I meant. The memories from that night replay in my mind again. It wasn't what I wanted, but does that really make it rape?

You assure me it does. You're talking about support groups and resources for victims, but certainly those things don't apply to me. I didn't even know I'd been raped. In fact, I'm still not really sure what happened to me qualifies as rape, no matter how many times you say that it does. The girls that need those support groups don't want someone like me there. They have real rapes they're trying to deal with.

You put some more words down on your notebook and promise me what happened to me is a real rape. But what happened to me? I had sex with my boyfriend at a party. Surely that happens all the time. Maybe if I hadn't been drinking, I would have actually stopped him. I would have told him I wasn't ready and that I wanted my first time to be somewhere else. I would have been more confident. It was my own fault for drinking that vodka drink.

When I tell you I wish I'd never drank that drink, you tell me that has nothing to do with what happened. But I think it does. Of course it does.

That was the first of many drinks. I didn't like the taste of the vodka, but Adam liked the taste of whiskey. We started going to more and more parties, and Adam would always get me vodka. He would drink whiskey until he got bored, and then he would lead me to a vacant room where we would have sex. Sometimes it was an empty bedroom, but when a bedroom wasn't available, he'd pull me into a bathroom and make me lean over the sink as he pushed into me from behind.

Once, when there was no bedroom available and someone was getting sick in the bathroom, Adam dragged me into a laundry room in a dark, unfinished basement.

I hated having sex at those parties. I hated that everyone knew why we were leaving the crowd, and I hated the way Adam would high-five his buddies when we would return to the party. I hated the way Adam would force my skirt up around my waist and push himself inside me. I hated everything about it. But I loved Adam, so I did it for him.

He wanted me to wear skirts to parties so it was easier to have sex. He'd text me and tell me to wear a skirt because we were going out. He'd put a winking emoji after the message. He'd tell me it was sexy that I would wear skirts for him, and he'd play with the hems as we drove to the parties. Then he would get our drinks, and I would nervously wait for the moment when he would put his cup down and drag me toward a vacant room.

I never told him no after the first time, but I still hated it. I started drinking more of the vodka Adam would get for me. It got easier to shut off my mind when Adam would pull me into dirty bathrooms or dingy laundry rooms with each sip of vodka I drank. I figured out if I drank enough, I couldn't actually feel Adam pushing himself inside me. I could almost pretend it wasn't happening. It was like I became numb from the waist down.

Although I still didn't like the taste, I started to craved that numbness the vodka provided.

CHAPTER THIRTY-FIVE

I started wanting the numb feeling vodka gave me all the time. I desperately wanted to not care about what was going on around me or inside of me. I wanted to feel disconnected all the time.

I guess that's really when things like school went off the rails for me. I worked so hard for so long to keep my grades high and to excel with my schoolwork, but it no longer seemed worth the effort. For so long I rushed to class and stressed about assignments and tests. Suddenly I found myself sitting in class, watching the other students taking notes and wondering why I used to care so much about my grades. I didn't even bother to listen to the lectures anymore. I'd once hung on every word my teachers said, searching for the underlying meaning and ways to apply it to other topics. Now the words drifted around me senselessly, making no impact on me whatsoever.

Almost a month into my full-body numbness, my English teacher pulled me aside after class.

"Sasha, has everything been alright lately? You haven't quite seemed yourself in class."

I always liked Mrs. Sampson, but I found her inquiry into my laziness intolerable. I stood slumped in front of her with my arms crossed over my chest, oozing the annoyance I was feeling.

Undeterred by my disinterest, Mrs. Sampson pressed on. The was concern in her eyes, which somehow annoyed me even more.

"It's just... I noticed you don't take notes anymore in class. Lately, I haven't even seen you with your notebook out."

She paused, searching my face. I stared back at her. I had nothing to say. There was no way I could make her understand how pointless her class seemed to me now.

Mrs. Sampson sighed, clearly frustrated at my unwillingness to communicate with her. I imagine she thought she'd be able to get through to me. She struck me as the type who believed she was changing the world, one student at a time.

"I'm worried about you, Sasha," she said finally.

I just shrugged. I couldn't explain to her why I was feeling so numb. Actually, if I'm being honest, I don't think I actually even knew why I was feeling it. I just wanted to walk away from her.

Mrs. Sampson sighed again, seeming to deflate.

"Just so you know, your grade is really suffering. It's a shame; you've always been such a wonderful student."

I stared down at the floor. She wanted answers, but I didn't have any to provide her. When I continued to say nothing, she shook her head.

I mumbled something about not wanting to be late for my next class and brushed past her. As I walked away, I heard her say something about Columbia and how I was throwing away my dream.

I hardly remembered that Columbia had once been my dream. It hadn't felt important in a long time. At one point in my life,

Columbia was the only thing that mattered to me. I tried to recall why, but I couldn't. That was the old Sasha's dream. The nerdy Sasha. The Sasha that didn't have Adam.

The only reason I kept going to school was to see Adam. As an athlete, his attendance at school was required. I spent all my time with him. He picked me up each morning before school, and we would be together until the bell rang, forcing us into our separate classes. In between, at lunch and in chemistry, Adam and I were together. After school, I would wait in his pickup truck until his practice was over, and then he would drive me home.

When we were together, I was happy to be with him. When Adam was happy, we would walk hand and hand through the hallways as if school were nothing more than an inconvenience. A place we wasted some time before we could go do something more fun. But when Adam was upset or angry, I felt like I was walking around holding the hand of a ticking time bomb. I never knew what little thing might set him off, and when he did explode, it was generally my fault.

I spent all my time and energy trying to please him in order to avoid the dark times when he was upset. It was amazing how his moods affected me. When he was happy, I felt lighter inside, and everything seemed bright and exciting. But when Adam was upset, the darkness would descend upon me, too. I'd feel heavy and weighed down, as if the sun might never shine again. I'd pray for numbness, in any form.

Although I tried to never upset Adam, whenever I did, the effects always seemed to last into the night. Adam would ignore my phone calls and text messages, leaving me alone in my despair.

On one particularly terrible evening, I found myself desperate for the numbness to take over. I tried calling Adam, but he silenced my calls, sending each one to voicemail before the first ring even finished. I knew I had no one to blame but myself. George had caught me after one of my classes. He'd grabbed my arm as he passed me and pulled me to the side of the hall.

"Why'd you stop taking pictures at the games?" He was still holding my arm. His touch was light, but I wrenched my arm away like he was burning me. I glanced over my shoulder, hoping Adam hadn't made it out of his classroom yet. George cocked his head. I mumbled something about my camera being broken. I couldn't tell George that Adam had forbidden it.

"Your pictures were really good. I miss getting a chance to see them. I can't even find you on Facebook anymore."

I shrugged, trying to think of an excuse. I was looking at the floor between George's sneakers. George touched my arm again and asked if I was alright.

"Why wouldn't she be alright?" I jumped at the sound of Adam's voice. George removed his hand from my arm and held it out to fist bump Adam. Adam ignored him and repeated his question.

"I was just wondering why she stopped taking pictures at our games, dude. She had some pretty awesome shots."

Adam's arm was around my waist and his fingers were digging into my hip bone.

"She decided she wanted to focus more on the game. She's there to watch me, after all."

George smiled, but he didn't look convinced. Overhead, the bell rang, and I was grateful to end the awkwardness.

Adam had been furious at me. Despite my insisting that George cornered me, he accused me of being a flirt. He hadn't spoken to me for the rest of the day.

With no one else to turn to, I found myself sitting alone in my kitchen. I wanted to slam my fists on the table and scream as loud as my lungs would let me.

Instead, I stood up to pace, taking long strides across the kitchen's tile floor. I paced from the doorway to the fridge and back again. As I turned to make another pass through the room, my gaze landed on the clear glass bottle of Absolut vodka my mother kept on top of the fridge. My mother drank occasionally, and when she did, she usually preferred wine, but this was the bottle she used to make cosmos when her best friend came over. The bottle was already open, and I could see the liquid inside.

I never drank outside of the parties I attended with Adam, and I'd never thought about drinking alone, but the bottle drew me toward it. Quietly, I reached up and pulled it down, cradling it in front of me. I'd never had Absolut vodka before. The brands at the parties were usually cheap and came in large plastic containers. The glass surrounding the Absolut felt heavy, despite its slim outline. I paused, holding the bottle and listening. I knew my mother wasn't home. She'd left an hour ago for a date with a man whose name she didn't bother to mention. I don't know what I was listening for, but I heard nothing. Taking that to be a sign, I carried the bottle over to the counter and took down a glass from the cabinet.

I poured the vodka into the glass, filling it nearly to the brim. I was careful to replace the bottle back exactly where I'd found it. I imagined my mother had no idea how much liquid was left inside, since it was used so infrequently. I carried the glass down the hall to my bedroom and placed it on my nightstand.

I checked my phone again, staring at the empty home screen with no new notifications. Adam had not called or texted. I felt a fresh pang through my chest. I reached for the glass on my nightstand and took a long sip, urging the numbness to come quickly. Surprisingly, the vodka didn't bite at the back of my tongue the way it usually did. I was able to quickly take additional sips. I imagined this was the smoothness I heard others talking about but had never experienced with the cheap vodka I was used to drinking.

I felt the warmth filling my belly and welcomed it. I knew the numbness would follow. I drank down the rest of the glass and lay back on my bed, waiting. I just didn't want to feel the pain anymore. I wanted to get to the next morning, where I imagined Adam would pick me up as if nothing had happened tonight. I was able to slip into sleep, and the vodka ushered in the new day. As expected, the next morning Adam acted as if nothing had happened.

The vodka helped me survive. It quickly became my coping mechanism for dealing with Adam's moods. I couldn't risk continuing to drink from the bottle on top of my fridge, though. I knew my mother would eventually notice if I drank all of it. Instead, I asked Adam to get me some. I told him I wanted to have my own, in case there wasn't any for me at one of the upcoming parties. He promised me there would always be vodka at the parties but said he liked the idea of having my own bottle for other times.

"For when we're feeling frisky," he said, squeezing my butt in his hand. I just smiled, hoping he didn't notice me flinch.

CHAPTER THIRTY-SIX

Don't start with the lecture about how alcohol isn't the solution. I've seen the PSAs. I know all about the dangers of drinking and how it can affect my development and all that shit they tell you.

I get it. But you know, at the time, it really did feel like a solution. The numbness was everything I needed it to be. I just didn't want to feel the pain anymore.

I don't know who Adam got the vodka from. It wasn't Absolut, which was disappointing. I liked the way the Absolut slipped down my throat like warm silk. The brand Adam got me wasn't as bad as some of the kinds I had tried at parties, though. I could sip it without having to hold my breath. I hid the bottle in the back of my dresser, behind the workout clothes I never wore. I wrapped it in a pair of gym shorts that looked like they would be two sizes too big for me now. I'd lost a considerable amount of weight, and I'd recently had to purchase new jeans so I wouldn't need to wear a belt.

Knowing the bottle was in my drawer was comforting. When Adam was angry with me, I would slip into my bedroom and twist the cap. After a few sips, I would feel the warmth rising from my stomach and I would know the numbness was on its way. I could wait out Adam's moods as long as I had my bottle.

Despite my social calendar being fuller than it had ever been, I spoke to almost no one but Adam and my mother. I learned it was significantly easier to avoid arguments with Adam if I didn't talk to other boys, even if it was only as friends. I let Adam answer for me when one of his friends asked me a question. If Adam left me alone and someone addressed me directly, I would try to answer as bluntly as possible. I would try to maintain a straight face and avoid showing any emotion, and then I would look around immediately to see if Adam had seen the interaction. I found it significantly easier to head off Adam's anger than to be blindsided by it.

When it came to my mother, it felt like all we did was talk about Adam. My mother adored him more than ever, and she never missed an opportunity to tell me so. She continued to constantly reminded me how lucky I was to have such an amazing boyfriend.

"If I had had a boyfriend like Adam when I was your age, I think my life would have turned out differently," she said one night.

"Which part?" I asked, uncomfortably aware she might be referring to the pregnancy that had resulted in the two of us sitting together at this very moment.

"Oh. Oh, no," my mother said, clearly realizing the implication. "No, not that. Not you. Of course, I don't want to change that. I just mean, maybe I would have found someone worthy of loving for longer than just a couple days."

My mother blushed, and I realized I very rarely saw her uncomfortable. She sipped the wine glass she'd been swirling in front of her.

"I just mean Adam is a lovely young man and you're very lucky, that's all."

I swallowed hard, guilt rising into my throat. Not for the first time, I wondered if I was really as lucky as everyone thought. It was wonderful to have someone like Adam to love me, but trying to be the perfect girlfriend was exhausting. I was starting to feel like something was wrong with me. I couldn't seem to keep him happy, nor could I seem to stop making mistakes. I felt undeserving and unworthy of him, and therefore increasingly guilty about the fact that we were together.

I watched other girls with their boyfriends and wondered how they kept their relationships looking so effortless. They never seemed to have the heated arguments Adam and I had regularly. Though, looking back on it, "arguments" doesn't seem like the right word. We never really argued. Adam would get mad and I would apologize. It was our cycle.

It never occurred to me that maybe that wasn't normal. I just assumed other girls were better at hiding the issues than I was. Maybe that came with experience. I never once stopped to consider maybe this wasn't how relationships were supposed to be.

The truth was, I'd never seen a relationship up-close, behind closed doors. My mother never brought her dates home, so I never had the chance to see how she acted around those men.

I'd never been exposed to any other relationships other than Mrs. and Mr. Attwood. Their relationship always seemed like a fairytale, and I've never doubted that it's perfect. They were high school sweethearts who got engaged right after graduation. Mr. Attwood joined the Navy and was at sea much of the time that Mrs. Attwood was in school. They wrote love letters back and forth for the whole four years. They got married in a picture-perfect spring ceremony three days after Mrs. Attwood graduated college.

I always loved watching Mrs. and Mr. Attwood together. Their love for one another is the type of stuff people write love stories about. But I'd never seen them behind closed doors. They must fight sometimes, right? When they do, is it the ugly type of angry that Adam gets? Do they look less like the fairy tale and more like a horror movie? How could I know? They don't write the love stories about the bad times. They don't show the horrible fights in the rom-coms.

I had to assume what Adam and I had was completely normal. Maybe we were doing everything right and this was just what being in a relationship was. I assumed I was just seeing the behind-the-scenes for the very first time.

I didn't associate my newfound love for vodka with Adam, though. I didn't think of drinking as something I did because of him. The alcohol was something I drank because of me, because I was a fuck-up. I used it to drown the pain and guilt and loneliness. I blamed those feelings on myself. I felt like I caused them and I wouldn't be feeling them if I was better. A better girlfriend, a better person, more deserving, more worthy. It was all my fault. Never once did I think to blame that on Adam.

Another benefit of the vodka was that it helped significantly with sex. I still hated the way sex felt, but I was positive that meant there was something wrong with me. I never associated that with Adam either. What type of girlfriend hates having sex with her boyfriend? I was embarrassed and ashamed, so I drank a little vodka out of my secret bottle every time Adam asked me to wear a skirt. If I drank enough to get that fuzzy, numb feeling, it was easier to pretend that I didn't hate having sex.

After I had finished the first bottle of vodka, I asked Adam to get me another one. We were talking on the phone one night after he dropped me off at the house. We'd had a good day and I was concerned about ruining it with my request. I asked quickly, hoping that catching him off guard might help avoid any type of fight. There was a painfully long silence after I asked, though, and I immediately knew my question would not be quickly breezed over.

"We haven't even had the chance to enjoy the bottle I got you together. Have you been drinking it with someone else?"

There was an edge in his voice and I knew this was a dangerous direction. I stared at the drawer where the empty bottle of vodka was tucked into the back. Knowing the bottle was empty made me panic. My mind raced for an explanation that might ward off Adam's anger.

"No, of course not. My mom found the other one. She took it

and dumped it out." I tried to make my lie sound as convincing as possible. I held my breath as I waited for Adam's reply.

"Oh," Adam said after a beat of silence. The edge had left his voice. "You should have hidden it better." I let out my breath in a quiet rush, feeling like I'd just managed to dodge a bullet.

"I know, I know. But I didn't expect her to come in and try to borrow clothes from me. I won't hide the next one in my dresser."

"Was she mad?" Adam seemed to find the imaginary situation comical.

"I told her it was Amanda's and I had taken it away from her. She said she always knew Amanda was a bad influence on me."

"Wow, that was smart. I'll see if Tony can pick you up another bottle this weekend. But you'll have to come up with a much better hiding spot this time."

As the conversation moved on, I was relieved. Although I felt pangs of guilt over lying to Adam, avoiding the crisis of having him mad at me when I didn't have any vodka seemed like a fair trade. It had only been a small lie, after all, and in reality, the truth wasn't actually that bad either. It's not like I'd been drinking the vodka with some other guy, as Adam had originally suspected. I argued to myself that the little lie was okay and I shouldn't feel too guilty about it. I also decided I would need to find my own source for getting future bottles of vodka so I didn't have to continue to lie to Adam about why I needed more. How do normal kids get alcohol? I had never even seen a fake ID. I would have to do some research into the topic.

CHAPTER THIRTY-SEVEN

Adam called a little while before he came to pick me up and told me he wanted me to wear his favorite jean skirt. It was the day before his eighteenth birthday. He told me his friends were throwing him a birthday party at John's house and he wanted me to look sexy.

I knew Adam would expect me to have sex with him. Even though we were now having sex at least once a week and I was taking the edge off it with the vodka, I still hadn't learned to like it.

I could never figure out what was so wrong with me. All everyone else could ever talk about was sex, so it has to be pretty great. But when Adam and I had sex, it just hurt. I'm not even sure which part is supposed to feel good. It always just felt like he was stabbing me. But I figured since Adam seemed to be enjoying his half, the problem was definitely with me. I never mentioned it to him because I didn't want him to realize there was anything wrong with me. When he would finish and say, "did you like that, babe?" I always told him yes.

I figured it didn't matter that I didn't like it. I would squeeze my eyes shut and just hope for it to be over as quickly as possible. It was easier if I had drunk a lot of vodka, though. Sometimes I wouldn't even have to close my eyes. If I drank enough, I could ignore what was happening between my legs altogether.

On the night before Adam's birthday, I put on the outfit he requested and slipped the bottle of vodka out of its hiding spot in the back of my dresser. I took two large sips from the bottle, letting the liquid burn down into my stomach. I was about to return the bottle to its hiding spot, when I decided I better have another long swig. I hoped the numbness would set in early.

Five minutes later, Adam's truck pulled up in front of my house, and I slid into the seat next to him. I could still feel the warmth in my belly, and it was just enough to make me feel a little bit silly when he told me how sexy I looked in my short skirt. He rested his hand on my thigh as he drove, and I could feel his thumb rubbing slow circles on my skin. When we arrived at John's, Adam immediately got me a cup of vodka. It was mixed with Pepsi, which was fine. I could drink it faster when the taste was masked by the sickly-sweet soda.

Adam refilled my cup three times throughout the night as I sat silently beside him and his friends. The numbness had set in just like I wanted, and I was feeling warm and content. I was happy to watch over Adam's shoulder as he played cards.

I knew that at some point, Adam would want to disappear into the upstairs bedroom, and I was nervous that the numbness might start to wear off before then. When Adam glanced over and saw that I was finishing off my fourth drink, he smiled and asked if I was ready for another. I held up my cup and he took it from me.

He reached for my hand and pulled me to my feet. I felt unsteady as I stood beside him, and the room seemed to be swaying from side to side, like the house was surrounded by water instead of land. I held tightly to Adam's hand as I followed him through the living room. His hand might have been the only thing keeping me on my feet.

Adam guided me to the makeshift bar where Tony was dutifully stationed and had my cup refilled. He placed it into my hands, and I took a sip instinctively. The drink tasted like it was only soda. I opened my mouth to complain about the missing vodka, but Adam was already leading me away from the bar.

Instead of returning to the card game, Adam led me upstairs. We had to take the stairs slowly because they seemed to be moving underneath my feet and I was having a hard time keeping track of where they were. Adam walked behind me with his hands on my hips, propelling me forward one step at a time.

When we finally reached the landing, Adam pulled me into the same room where we'd had sex for the first time. I set my cup down on the dresser and prepared for Adam to lift my skirt up and push himself inside me.

I turned around to find Adam staring at me, his pants already unbuttoned. I remember I could see the bulge of blue boxers pushing out from behind his jeans. I remember he stepped toward me. I remember he leaned in to kiss me.

But I don't remember anything else.

No matter how hard I focus my memory, no matter how much I think about that night, I can't force my mind to remember what happened next. No images or feelings come to mind. There's just darkness.

The first thing I remember is feeling cold. I don't remember falling asleep, but I must have. I opened my eyes, shivering and looked down at my naked body. I was lying on top of that white comforter, alone in the bedroom. I don't remember taking my clothes off or climbing up onto the bed.

I was so confused, seeing my pale skin against the stark white comforter. I sat up in a panic, but the sudden motion made the room spin and my stomach lurch. I held my hand over my mouth, willing myself not to throw up. When the feeling passed and the room seemed to steady itself, I looked around. I remembered coming upstairs with Adam, but I realized he was gone.

Gingerly, I eased myself out of bed. Not only was the room starting to spin again, but I realized I was sore. The pain between my legs reminded me of the time when I was very young and had fallen on the balance beam at gymnastics. I landed straddling the beam, and my coach told me I was lucky I hadn't fractured my pelvis. I didn't know what my pelvis was at the time. I couldn't remember falling, but now my body hurt as if I had.

My mouth felt like I'd been chewing on cotton balls. I looked around, desperate for a drink of water. There was a cup on the bedside table I vaguely recalled placing down. I picked the cup up and took a small sip, instantly aware I made a mistake. The combination of too sweet soda and cheap vodka made me gag. I dropped to my knees and retched into the small trashcan beside the bed. I spit acidic bile on top of the used condoms that were inside. When my stomach was empty, I sat back on my heels, panting. A cold sweat covered my body, and I shivered again.

I was suddenly aware I was still naked and instinctively hugged my arms around my bare chest as I forced myself to my feet. I found my clothes scattered around the floor of the room in tangled balls. I slowly got dressed using nearby furniture to steady myself. In the pocket of my skirt, I found my cell phone. I clicked it on to check the time and nearly dropped it when I saw how late it was. The screen displayed 3:30 in the morning. Both Adam and I had a midnight curfew. I couldn't believe it was so late.

I immediately clicked the icon for text messages, which housed several angry messages from my mother. It was clear her initial worry about me being late had degraded to anger, as her last message declared if I came home alive, I was going to be grounded until I was dead. My stomach lurched uneasily as I thought about having to face my mother's wrath when I returned home.

There were also multiple messages from Adam. The first one arrived at a quarter to eleven.

r u up yet?

sasha we need to go

i can't be late for curfew

sasha???

There was a gap in the time between this message and the next. About the amount of time it would take for him to drive home from John's house. Then the messages started again at about 12:10.

i tried to wake u up and u wouldnt. i couldnt wait for u anymore.

u'll have to get a ride home with someone else

r u still asleep?

u better not be with anyone else

ur such a whore. i know ur sleeping with john

fuck u and fuck him

i can't believe u ruined my birthday like this

what the fuck Sasha

bitch

I had no idea what Adam was talking about. I couldn't remember anything. I closed my eyes and thought as hard as I could, but the last thing I could remember was Adam moving toward me. Everything went black after that. The realization that Adam had left me at John's house slowly took hold of my mind. I had no way of getting home. He left me essentially in a stranger's house on the other side of town.

I didn't know what to do. I tried calling Adam's phone, but it went straight to voice mail. I called over and over again, but his voice mail message was the only thing that ever answered me. Around four in the morning, I hesitantly opened the bedroom door and walked toward the stairs. There were still lights on downstairs, and I could hear the drone of a television show coming from somewhere below me. I carefully worked my way down the stairs, gripping the banister tightly.

Once I was in the entryway, I could see a couple of bodies sprawled out randomly on the living room furniture. In the dim light, I couldn't tell who they were, but I was certain I didn't want to wake them. As quietly as I could, I moved toward the front door and slipped out into the cool night air. The fog was heavy, and I could feel its damp weight in my hair and on my skin. I walked down the road on autopilot, but when I reached Main Street, I burst into tears. It would take me over an hour to walk home, and my stomach and head were aching. I sat down on the curb and put my head between my knees.

After a few shaky breaths, I reached for my phone and called my mother. She answered on the first ring, and I knew she hadn't been sleeping. A pang of guilt shot through my pounding head.

"Sasha?" Her voice was sharp, and my name came out as both a question and a statement. I inhaled a deep breath and tried to hide my tears.

"Mom." My voice was barely a whisper. I was aware again of how dry my throat was, and the word came out raspy and sounded foreign. "Can you come get me?"

There was a beat of silence on the other end of the phone, and I imagined my mother rubbing her forehead with her fingers.

"Where are you?" She emphasized each word, spitting them out through what I imagined were gritted teeth.

"The corner of Main Street and Sentinel Road."

"Don't move," she said, and the phone went dead.

I sat on the curb taking deep breaths until I heard the sound of my mother's Nissan pulling up in front of me. I wobbled as I got to my feet and collapsed into the passenger side of the car. My mother's stare was almost painful. I nearly choked on the first sob, and when she didn't offer me any comfort, I broke down completely. My mother watched me cry for a minute and then silently steered the car back onto the road.

When we arrived home, she got out of the car and slammed the door, not even bothering to look back at me. I sat in the car trying to collect myself for what felt like an hour. When I finally poured myself out of the car and into the house, my mother was waiting for me in the entryway.

"Don't even think about leaving this house for the next two weeks. I can't even look at you right now. Get your drunken ass up to your bedroom."

I heaved myself up the stairs and collapsed into my bed. I was sobbing again, though at that point I didn't even know why. I watched my room start to fill with light from the sunrise. At some point, I must have dozed off, but I don't remember when. All I know is, for once, waking up didn't seem to fix anything at all.

CHAPTER THIRTY-EIGHT

My whole body hurt when I woke up later that morning. My head ached and my stomach felt like I'd been battling the flu. There was still pain between my legs, and it hurt to move. The sunlight made my eyes burn, and it felt like I was trying to swallow glass. The clock on my bedside table said it was almost noon, but it felt as though I'd only been asleep for a few minutes.

I didn't want to get out of bed. I didn't want to face my mother. I didn't want to talk to Adam. I reached for my phone and immediately regretted doing so. There was a new onslaught of messages from him. He demanded to know where I was and why I wasn't answering him. He accused me of intentionally ruining his birthday. His last message simply read that I was the worst girlfriend ever.

I dropped the phone back onto my nightstand and pushed myself out from the safety of my bed. I nervously started toward the kitchen, where I expected to find my mother waiting for me. I don't know if it was better or worse to find the kitchen empty. The door to my mother's bedroom was closed, and I didn't know if she was in there avoiding me or if she was still trying to catch up on the sleep I prevented her from getting the night before.

I took down a cup and guzzled water from the faucet. I soaked a paper towel and laid it on the back of my neck as I leaned over the sink. I tried to work my mind through the events of the night before, but I was still finding black holes where my memories should be.

Of course, I know what happened now, but at the time, I couldn't figure out why my mind went blank as soon as I started trying to remember having sex with Adam. I wanted to make sure the numbness lasted through the evening, and in a way, I'd been successful. I'd drunk enough to bring me to the point of blacking out and then passing out, an experience I'd never had before.

My mother didn't talk to me for the rest of the day. When she finally came out of her bedroom, she didn't even acknowledge my presence in the kitchen. She just came out, got a cup of coffee, and disappeared down the hall again. I waited the rest of the afternoon for her to come back out, but she remained locked up in her room.

By dinner time, I was actually desperate to talk to her, even if it meant she was going to yell at me. I needed someone to talk to. I wanted to tell her what happened. I wanted to ask what was wrong with me. I wanted to feel like I wasn't all alone.

But I was alone.

I had no one to talk to. Not even my own mother.

I tried calling Adam in the early afternoon, but he ignored my call and the subsequent texts I sent him. His final message, the one saying I was the worst girlfriend ever, was all I could think about.

The loneliness felt like a tangible thing, something I could physically feel weighing me down. I dragged it with me up to my bedroom, where I stared at the blank screen of my phone.

I missed Grandma June. I felt like if she was still here, I would have been able to talk to her. She would have known what to do. But she wasn't here. I hadn't even had the opportunity to say goodbye to her. I tried to push her memory out of my mind. I knew she'd be disappointed in the failure that I'd become. I was failing at school, I was failing as a girlfriend, and I'd failed as a daughter. There was nothing left of the girl Grandma June had once been so proud of.

I thought about Amanda and how I'd always been able to reach out to her when I needed someone to talk to. It'd been months now since I'd last spoken to her. I'd seen her recently in school, but only in passing. She hadn't bothered to acknowledge me either.

As I lay there in the dark, I thought about the other friends I used to talk to. I'd never been the most social person, but I would talk to Amanda and Maura and Andrew a few times a day. I would laugh at the funny pictures they would send to my Facebook page and read the seemingly never-ending group text messages that would bounce around throughout the week.

I hadn't spoken to any of them in ages. I spent all my time with Adam and his friends, and I realized now that meant I didn't have time to see any of my friends. I hadn't noticed when the text messages from Maura and Andrew stopped coming in, but I felt their absence now. I thought about sending one of them a text, but I didn't even know what I would say. I figured we weren't even friends anymore.

Even the distance between me and my mother felt astronomical. I wanted to go and curl up in her bed the way I used to when I was a child. I wanted her to tell me everything was going to be alright, but I knew that wasn't the case. It didn't feel like anything was going to be alright ever again.

I didn't know if Adam and I were still together, and to be honest, I wasn't sure which was worse. Life with Adam in it had become so complicated. As much as I loved Adam, I missed how simple my life had been before we were together. But when I thought about life without him, I realized I didn't have anything left. Without Adam, I would have no one. I would be stuck in this loneliness forever.

I lay in the dark with my mind buzzing. My body hurt; my brain hurt. I wanted it all to stop. I wanted it all to be easy. I thought about the bottle in the back of my dresser, but vodka had betrayed me. The numbness led to this loneliness and pain.

If my vodka wasn't the answer, I didn't know what was.

Although I still felt foggy, my mind raced through thoughts faster than I could process them. I hated myself at that moment. I hated who I was. I didn't even know who I was, but I hated her. I hated the loneliness. I hated that Amanda had left me alone. I hated that Adam had left me alone. Everyone had left me. I hated that I was so easily abandoned, so easily forgotten.

I was a disappointment to my mother. I'd let her down and she hated me now, too. If your boyfriend stopped loving you, and you had no friends, and even your mother didn't love you, what was the point of being alive?

And that's when I thought it. That's when the thought slid into my head and got stuck there. I didn't want to be alive. I wanted to be permanently numb.

Everything seemed to click into place once the thought was there. Everything made so much more sense. It was as if the fog had lifted to show me the light. I knew what I had to do. I knew how to make the numbness come.

CHAPTER THIRTY-NINE

The exact wording of that last message to Amanda doesn't really matter. What matters is I told her she was right. I figured it didn't matter that at that point we hadn't spoken in months. In what I thought was going to be my last moment, all that mattered to me was telling her she was right and I was sorry.

I actually don't know why I decided to send the message. It wasn't for attention, even though I know people whispered about it after the fact. I certainly didn't expect her to save me. In the moment, it just seemed important to get it all off my chest, to tell her how wrong I was about everything and beg her to forgive me some day. Maybe a part of me also wanted someone to know the truth about all the pain I was carrying around inside me.

I poured my heart out in that message. I told her about how hard it was to deal with Adam's anger and how horrible a girlfriend I was. I told her that no matter how hard I tried, I couldn't stop myself from fucking everything up. I told her I wished I could take back the awful things I had said to her that day in the hallway. I told her she was still my best friend and I was sorry for everything.

I didn't wait for a response. I said my piece and then turned off my phone. I didn't need it anyway. I hadn't really needed it in months. There was no one I communicated with anymore; there was no one else to say goodbye to. Adam had stripped me of everyone. I had been completely absorbed into his atmosphere, and now that I was without him, there was nothing left.

I had allowed him to shut me out from the rest of the world. I was so angry at myself for that. There was so much I hated myself for allowing. But in the end, I didn't blame Adam for this situation. I blamed myself. I hated myself.

Despite everything, I was still madly in love with Adam. I think I knew I shouldn't be, deep down, but I couldn't just turn off the feelings for him. He's Adam Lincoln, after all. Everyone loves him. I still loved him then, and maybe I even still do.

I couldn't picture my life without him. I couldn't imagine living in a world where I had no one.

I made the decision that seemed like the easiest way to end all the pain. It seemed so practical in that moment. In fact, I didn't see any other option at all. When I made the decision, when I finally realized it was my way out, I actually felt calm. I wasn't scared or worried. Instead, I felt like I'd finally found the perfect solution.

I went to the bathroom and opened the medicine cabinet. On the shelf in front of me was an array of bottles, tubes and jars. Toward the back, I spotted the forgotten bottle of pain killers my mother had used after a car accident years earlier. The bottle stood collecting dust behind tubes of lipstick and jars of facial cream. I carefully removed it from the shelf and slipped back into my bedroom.

I stood calmly at my dresser. I removed the child-proof cap from the bottle and eyed the pills inside. I wasn't sure how many were necessary to overdose. I counted at least twelve. I assumed that would be enough.

Without much more thought, I tipped the little orange prescription bottle up so that the tiny round pills tumbled into my mouth. I washed them down with what was left in the bottle of vodka. Even though my stomach was still unsettled from the night before, the vodka felt warm and familiar as it slid down my throat. I'm not sure why, but I tucked the pill bottle and the empty vodka container back into the drawer.

I felt warm as I settled myself into my bed and tucked my covers around myself for the last time. I lay back onto my pillow and allowed myself to fall asleep.

No, I didn't leave a note.

There was nothing left to say.

***

When I woke up a few hours later in the bright hospital room, I was honestly confused. A man wearing green scrubs was standing with his back to me, checking one of the many beeping machines beside me. My tongue felt too big for my mouth and I was aware of how dry it was. I asked the man for a drink. My voice came out raspy and was barely a whisper.

The man jumped a little like he hadn't realized I was in the room with him. When he turned to face me, he smiled and had kind eyes. He was much older than I'd originally thought. Deep wrinkles creased his forehead. He asked if there was anything else I needed. I shook my head, because saying anything else seemed too hard.

The man patted my arm where it was lying motionless on top of the hospital blankets. He promised to get me some water and let my family know I was awake.

He paused in the doorway and added, "And we'll find you someone to talk to about those boy problems of yours."

After he left the room, I thought back on everything that had happened over the past few months. Was that really all this amounted to? Common, everyday "boy problems"?

Amanda and I always thought "boy problems" came from not

having a boyfriend. For years, "boy problems" had been liking someone who didn't like you back or trying to get attention from a boy who was never going to notice you. I never imagined there were worse boy problems, problems that came from actually having the boyfriend.

I was still thinking about this when my mother and Amanda came though the curtain covering the doorway of my room. They both immediately began fussing over me and talking at once, and after so much time feeling completely alone, I was overwhelmed by them. Part of me wanted them to leave, but the other part of me was terrified they would.

It turns out that, after I turned my phone off, Amanda tried to call me. When her calls kept going straight to my voice mail, she had a bad feeling something was wrong. She called my mom, who found me unconscious in my bedroom. I was rushed to the hospital, where they pumped my stomach shortly before I woke up. Amanda and my mother had been there the whole time.

I know you already know this part. This is how we ended up here together. You were the lucky person they scrounged up to "listen to my boy problems." There was lots of "concern for my well-being." Lots of talk about whether I was "a danger to myself or others." Suddenly, after months of feeling like I barely talked at all, I'm surrounded by lots of talking.

You want to know how I feel now, after sharing my story with someone. I know you're really asking if I still want to off myself. At the end of the day, that's why we're really here, isn't it?

It's a valid question, though, I suppose, since I did already try it. I guess the answer is… I don't know.

At the time, I thought there was no other way out of the hole Adam buried me in. I couldn't see the light anymore. I didn't think I could live without Adam, but I guess I've survived so far. Then again, I've been here with you, so there really wasn't any other choice.

I'm not the old Sasha anymore, and I don't think there's any going back to her. The old Sasha was naïve and believed in true love and happy endings. If I'm being totally honest, I don't know if I can believe in those things anymore.

You're not going to tell me what you're writing and whether you think I'm still suicidal.

"Let's see how things progress," you say as you close your notebook.

Progress.

I guess that's what this is.

Progress.

For more information about preventing teen dating violence,
please visit

www.ThatsNotCool.com

www.ingramcontent.com/pod-product-compliance
Lightning Source LLC
Chambersburg PA
CBHW030741110726
47900CB00008B/2401

* 9 7 8 0 5 7 8 8 9 3 8 4 6 *